WINNING AT WORK

Anu Kaushal Manhotra is one of the most well-known names in the field of corporate and teacher training. She is known for her contribution on 'values and moral education', a subject on which she has written in detail in her debut book *Wake up to VAKE: A Trainer's Love Story*. She has been associated with various schools, colleges, universities and MNCs to groom youngsters for success in the professional world. She is also known for her witty and small poems.

She started writing to reach out to more people, and has written many articles for teachers and corporate professionals in various magazines.

This is her third book, which is crafted with her vast experience and knowledge in the field of communications and soft skills.

Praise for the book

The human mind needs to be trained and equipped with a set of skills to enable it to fruitfully engage and excel in today's complex and intense world seamlessly interconnected in this industrial age.

This book provides you with such knowledge and skills to succeed in life.

—*Mr Sandeep Toor*
Plant Head, Hawkins Cookers Ltd, Hoshiarpur

Another wonderful compilation of effective Dos & Don'ts for young professionals aspiring to see themselves in the boardroom at some point of time in their life.

This book provides tips on power dressing, communication skills, handling board/staff meetings, including conference calls, etc., which are sine qua non in the contemporary corporate world.

—*Dr J.K. Gulati*
Associate Professor-cum-Convener,
University Business School, G.N.D. University, Jalandhar

**UNLEASHING THE POWER OF
CONFIDENCE AND SELF-DISCIPLINE**

WINNING AT WORK

Anu Kaushal Manhotra

RUPA

Published by
Rupa Publications India Pvt. Ltd 2021
7/16, Ansari Road, Daryaganj
New Delhi 110002

Sales centres:
Bengaluru Chennai
Hyderabad Jaipur Kathmandu
Kolkata Mumbai Prayagraj

Copyright © Anu Kaushal Manhotra 2021

All rights reserved.
No part of this publication may be reproduced, transmitted,
or stored in a retrieval system, in any form or by any means,
electronic, mechanical, photocopying, recording or otherwise,
without the prior permission of the publisher.

The views and opinions expressed in this book are the author's own and
the facts are as reported by her which have been verified to the extent
possible, and the publishers are not in any way liable for the same.

P-ISBN: 978-93-89967-81-4
E-ISBN: 978-93-89967-82-1

Fifth impression 2025

10 9 8 7 6 5

The moral right of the author has been asserted.

Printed in India

This book is sold subject to the condition that it shall not,
by way of trade or otherwise, be lent, resold, hired out, or otherwise
circulated, without the publisher's prior consent, in any form of
binding or cover other than that in which it is published.

I dedicate this book to all my trainees, my co-travel(l)ers, in the journey called sharing and learning

Contents

Preface — ix

1. How to Brand Yourself — 1
2. How to Power Dress — 15
3. How to Promote Yourself — 27
4. How to Communicate at Work — 34
5. How to Write Professional Emails — 40
6. How to Make and Attend Conference Calls — 48
7. How to Conduct a Meeting — 53
8. How to Handle Lunch or Dinner Meetings — 61
9. How to Put Colleagues and Business Associates at Ease — 73
10. How to Build a Positive Corporate Culture — 80
11. How to Keep the Passion Going — 91
12. How to Negotiate — 95
13. How to Set Goals — 102
14. How to Create Workplace Dos and Don'ts — 110
15. How to Do SWOT Analysis — 113
16. How to Lead — 116
17. How to Learn and Stay Ahead — 123
18. How to Answer Top HR Questions — 128
19. How to Handle Appraisals — 144
20. How to Improve Your GQ — 148
21. How to Get Smarter Quicker — 151

Preface

This book is for you—whether you are a young professional or a seasoned one, whether you wish to step on to the next level or reach new heights.

The main purpose of this book is to share some simple and classy ways to stay happy at your workplace. This book will provide practical guidance. It contains worksheets and exercises, which will help you acquire skills and enhance your self-esteem.

This book will also be very useful for corporate and soft skills trainers because it is designed in a simple manner to help understand tactics and latest strategies to excel at the modern workplace.

1

How to Brand Yourself

> *All of us need to understand the importance of branding. We are CEOs of our own companies: Me Inc. To be in business today, our most important job is to be head marketer for the brand called You.*
>
> —Tom Peters in *Fast Company*

Personal Image Management

In the professional world, I have noticed that people are very good at two things that are not quite professional: first, to judge others and second, to label them as something they may not be. So as a true professional, you need to be able to do this before anyone else does it for you. After all, when *you* have a chance to create beautiful art and write an amazing story, why let others do it?

In the modern business world, it is very crucial to stay ahead, and be confident and smart. You are no longer just an employee working within the four walls of your company, but also a professional working and interacting with counterparts, clients, etc., from across the world. So, in order to make a greater impact as a professional, why not craft a powerful personal image? This is important because when you invest in your branding, you project a positive image of yourself and your organization forever. In short, it is like creating a great legacy, which will stay even when you are gone.

As you begin to comprehend and appreciate the magnitude

of your personal image, you must set out on a deeper journey by asking two very important questions.

Why Do I Want to Create a Personal Image?

This is the most important question you as a professional should ask yourself. If you are not sure of 'what you do' or 'why you do' something, then there is no authenticity in your work and you may end up creating an image that is false or simply created for a namesake.

Simon Oliver Sinek, a well-known motivational speaker and an organizational consultant, rightly mentions that a great leader will always start their journey by asking, 'Why', as it gives them reason to forge ahead on their journey with great passion. Not just this, it also gives stakeholders and others an opportunity to stay connected with them and their passion for a very long time. Sinek calls this the Golden Circle.

Asking 'Why' is thus the first step towards creating a powerful personal image.

What Image Do I Create?

Always remember that you do not want to create an image of you that you are *not* or one that does not talk about the *real* you. When you are trying to build your image, keep the following key points in mind:

1. Bring to light your inner strength and present it to the world around you.
2. Try not to create an image that already exists; just be you and you will be able to carry it off very well.
3. Create a unique image. When you stay true to yourself, you create an image that has never been crafted before. This is because we are all unique and have different experiences that make us the people we are today. So, create a unique

image by tapping on all your personal learnings, and when you do that, you will set out on a journey of reinventing yourself.

Once you answer these two questions, you can proceed to understand your current personal image, how people perceive you and how you present yourself to them.

What Is Your Brand Image?

As a professional, you must be aware of your own backpack, if I may call it so. This means that you must be aware of the image you carry because it is something that follows you wherever you go. Your 'identity backpack' may contain a lot of self-confidence and assertiveness, but there are chances of this being perceived as arrogance by your peers. Thus, it is always a good idea to check, communicate and get feedback from others on a regular basis.

Since this feedback will help you improve your image, it is important to have good communication skills.

Let us check out a simple and fun exercise that will help you to know what you think of yourself viz-a-viz what others think of you. Let's begin the fun activity!

1. You need 3–4 colleagues or your managers.
2. You need a piece of paper and a pen.

Step 1: Take a sheet of paper and a pen and write down a few lines about yourself or rate yourself on a scale of 1 to 5, with 5 being the highest. Rate yourself on the basis of the following parameters that are used to gauge professionalism.

- Professional knowledge
- Communication skills
- Behaviour (or attitude) at work

Rate yourself on these three parameters (and you might add a few more as per your requirement). Do not show it to your colleagues—simply mention the score or write a line about yourself against each parameter and keep it to yourself.

Step 2: Ask your colleagues or managers to also rate you on these parameters.

Step 3: Collect those scores and do a small comparative analysis.

Step 4: Look out for any major differences, and if there are any then you can start working on those areas for improvement. Remember that the purpose behind this activity is to check your professional image against your professional setting. In other words, it is to see if your image is well in sync with your job title. For example, a doctor is expected to wear a sparkling white coat at the hospital, no matter how much of a style icon he/she may be in his/her personal life.

Quick Tips to Create a Power Image

Follow these tips and get ready to begin a journey towards a more beautiful you, inside out.

1. *Think beautiful:* You are nothing but your thoughts. Everything that happens in your life is the result of your thoughts, so when you are a positive thinker, you are sure to earn brownie points! So, be it in the professional arena or in your personal life, all you need to do is stay calm, be positive and live in the moment.
2. *Find the right words:* You should strive to enrich your vocabulary of positive words—the more positive words in your dictionary, the more positive and luckier you get. So, add more positive words when you communicate.
   For instance, if I ask you to quickly jot down ten words

to describe how you feel when you achieve something or succeed in your purpose, what kind of words come to your mind?

Hope you list at least 5 or 6 positive words—if not, it is time to start building up your positive-words vocabulary! If you can draw up 10, kudos to you!

3. *Know your USP:* Know what makes you a real and an authentic 'YOU'.

    As you are well aware, USP stands for unique selling point. You would have come across this word for various products and services, but have you ever wondered that as an individual, you too have your USP. So, what is that special quality that separates you from the rest of the world?

    It is time to think about it seriously. When you really know your USP, you can then show the world that conviction can move mountains, but if you do not believe in yourself and if you have never introspected, then you are just one in a pack, and nobody wants to be with an 'anybody'.

    Ask yourself: What is my USP? Why am I right for this task? Why am I perfect for this job? Be very clear, and this clarity comes only when you are self-aware.

4. *Visual image:* How do you look? Great, confident, manager-like or just regular?

It is sad but true that we are judged for the way we look, the way we dress up and carry ourselves. Most of us debate that visual image is not something that should be given much importance, but like it or not, it holds immense power. The good news however is that we can all learn to work upon it and improve it.

There are three critical elements to remember here:

1. Be well groomed
2. Wear clean and tidy clothes
3. Be aware of your body language

Be well-groomed

HSN Rule: This is the golden rule that I follow. When it comes to attaining that professional look, all you have to do is to focus on three things.

H = Hair
S = Skin
N = Nails

Hair: To get that classy look, girls must tie their hair; never leave it open as it is difficult to handle loose hair at a workplace where you have a lot to handle than just your hair!

Light or non-greasy hair oil is always better than no hair oil at all; never go to the workplace with dry hair! Having said that, it is advisable to apply very little oil, and one without a strong scent, as some people may be allergic to strong fragrances.

Always keep a comb. This applies to both men and women. It is a good idea to brush your hair, especially after lunch break. People with dishevelled hair leave a bad impression.

Skin: Healthy skin and daily showers go hand in hand. While you may invest a lot in buying expensive and branded clothes, if you do not take care of your personal hygiene, it is a waste of time and money.

Stay away from dirt and smell as body odour will make it unpleasant for your colleagues to be around you. Remember that it is not the colour of your skin but how you smell that makes all the difference.

What about perfume? Should you wear perfume to work? This is not a simple question to answer because many organizations have strict grooming etiquettes.

It is important to understand that strong perfumes can trigger allergies in others near you. Keep these points in mind when applying perfume when going to work.

1. Perfume is not something to be drenched in; just dab it or spray it. When you spray perfume, keep the bottle at least 25–30 cm away from your skin.
2. Perfume is to be applied on your pulse points. Because they are the warmest parts of your body, they react naturally to the perfume and smell the best. So go ahead and dab some on your wrists and behind your ears. But remember, only dab!
3. Pick a perfume that is mild as you are going to work—not to attend a party.
4. Do not rub the perfume after spraying it on your skin. For instance, if you apply perfume to your wrists, do not rub them together. Since they are pulse points, they are warm already. Also, when you rub your wrists against each other, you cause them to overheat and this can deteriorate the fragrance. It can also cause skin allergies.
5. Remember that perfumes work better on moisturized skin—not dry skin.

A word of caution is warranted here. As every individual has a unique body odour, what may be good for one may not work for another. So it is a good idea to try out different perfumes and select the one that suits you and your skin type the best.

Nails: For gentlemen, the simple rule is to keep nails short and dirt-free.

For some women, nails are just another way of accessorizing themselves. So let us talk about a clean-cut office look, rather than going crazy with the blues and greens.

Follow these simple rules when it comes to nail paints:

- Use a nude shade.
- Go for a French manicure. All classy women do this manicure. For this look, choose a pale pink or clear base coat and make the tips of your nails pop with a crescent of white nail polish.
- Beige is always in when it comes to nail polish.

Wear clean clothes

I strongly believe that staying simple will always remain in style; however, staying ignorant about key elements of style might make you look out of place at the workplace. When you enter the world of work—your professional arena—you dress up according to your industry and job profile. This is called power dressing.

Research on how and what to match with what, and what kind of accessories to use while at work. This information will help you walk into your office with more confidence. This will also help you with job interviews.

Remember, power dressing has a major impact on your career. Invest a little bit of time and money in wearing the right kind of clothes and accessories. For instance, it is always good to save some money to invest in a few good accessories and stationery items:

- Standard ball point pen
- Diary
- Wallet/handbag
- Wrist watch

- Good-quality belt
- Comfortable formal footwear

These need not be too expensive, but of good quality. Once you have this checklist ready, you will surely save and invest in something good that will help you look like a true professional. These accessories are not meant to show off, but create a good impression at the workplace.

Be aware of your body language

Let us talk about the third element of 'Visual Image'—the power of body language.

Let us focus on power postures here. This section will also give you a few tips that will not just help you look like a professional, but also make you feel like a superstar at work. Let us dive deep into understanding these invaluable tips.

Hand gestures

The number one power posture tip lies in your own hands. Literally! Most of us underestimate the use of hand gestures while speaking and instead give a lot of importance to eye contact when it comes to connecting with people, but the truth is, if you use hand gestures to support your words while speaking, you will sound more trustworthy.

It is very natural in some cases to use hand gestures as you speak. I too find it impossible to talk without using hand gestures. Of course, you must not overdo it as it looks weird; gesticulate to only support your words. These hand gestures make you look more trustworthy and honest, and it is more likely that people will listen to you then.

For instance, when I have to tell the audience that I have two important details to share, I use my hands to show the number because the corresponding gesture will help people listen and also retain that for longer because I supported verbal information with a hand gesture.

Hand gestures are also very powerful to convey your emotions, especially when you are short of words.

There are two very important and powerful hand gestures that can be used effectively.

A. Steeple your hands

Hand steeple position

This picture shows the 'hand steeple', in which the fingers are making a little 'rooftop'. This gesture shows confidence and authority, and is very popular with authority figures.

B. Keep your thumbs up

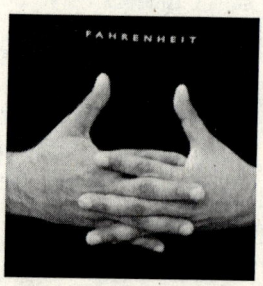

Thumbs up position

This gesture also shows authority and power. However, please bear in mind the cultural contexts when using this gesture because in some cultures, thumbs up is considered rude.

Acknowledgement

Remember that when you communicate, you are not just talking but also listening—and when you listen, you must acknowledge.

Acknowledging is a simple way of letting others know: 'Hey! I am with you and I am listening to you.'

As the first duty of love is to listen, love the speaker and acknowledge them by 'listening'. You can do this by nodding or tilting your head when you are listening to a speaker at a huge gathering, at a training workshop or even at business meetings (where you are a part of an audience). You should always contribute to these gatherings and meetings by nodding and also occasionally leaning slightly forward, in order to show that you listen well. This also makes you connect better with the speaker. In a face-to-face communication scenario in a group or with another person, you can support these gestures with small acknowledging words like 'Ah Ha', 'Okay', 'I understand', and so on. These small words and gestures will take you a long way in connecting with the speaker.

You can actually infuse and imbue more energy to big gatherings and dull meetings at the workplace if you are acknowledging the speaker well. So, do contribute even as a listener, and be a great one at that!

Upright posture

Having an upright posture is very crucial, and it goes without saying that good posture makes you look great, assertive and confident. Though it is not always easy to maintain it during long working hours, you can follow a few practices to avoid bad posture at work because not only does it make you look lazy, it might also have a detrimental effect on your health.

So make it a habit of getting up from your workstation every hour or so and just walk a few steps to relax your body. This helps you stay fit and active.

Another thing that helps a good and upright posture is improving workstation ergonomics.

Eye contact

Eyes are often called the windows to the soul. So, without a doubt, eye contact is a very strong non-verbal signal. In fact, it is the most talked-about element of non-verbal language.

While there is no denying this fact, do remember that too much eye contact is also considered inappropriate and unprofessional. Going overboard with it will not just make the other person uncomfortable but also ruin your chances of being known as a true professional.

When we talk about eye contact, it is necessary to understand that eye contact along with the bridging technique is the most powerful technique of conveying a message. So, what is the bridging technique?

- In simple words, it means that you should look at the mid-forehead of the person you are conversing with.
- You can begin by imagining a small triangle with its base beneath the eyes, the tip at the middle of the forehead, and the centre of the triangle on the bridge of the nose.
- While you speak you should focus 50 per cent of the time on the bridge of the nose. It is okay to move the gaze to the forehead or eyes occasionally. This technique will make you feel comfortable (and you

will listen like a thorough professional too) and also ensure that the speaker is at ease.
- Avoid looking at the lower half of the speaker's face during the business conversation. It is not considered a professional gaze.
- Also, a key element in eye contact that most of us tend to ignore is culture. While most of us know that it is appropriate to maintain eye contact with business colleagues from the West, it is not considered a sign of trustworthiness to look directly while speaking to a business associate—especially if they are seniors—from the Orient.

Your notes

How important is body language at the workplace? What are the few points that you found really interesting and intriguing in this section.

1.

2.

3.

4.

5.

Write a few lines about the concept of 'HSN' that you learnt in this chapter.

_____
_____
_____
_____
_____
_____
_____
_____
_____
_____
_____
_____

2

How to Power Dress

What you wear is how you present yourself to the world, especially today, when human contacts are so quick. Fashion is instant language.

—Miuccia Prada

Power dressing is the unique style of an individual that conveys position and authority in business or at the workplace. We all know the power of words and body language; however, sometimes we tend to overlook the power of our dressing sense—an aspect that has greater impact than we imagine.

As a true professional, you must not ignore this element. Also, since it is easy to adopt, why not learn about it rather than run away from it!

I have heard many people say that they believe in dressing simply. While this will always remain in style, staying ignorant of basic dressing rules is foolhardy. For example, what should be worn with a pair of black trousers? Can you wear white socks? This kind of confusion spells disaster and will only end up with you looking grossly out of place.

When people advise you to dress appropriately for your dream position, what they mean is dressing better or power dressing, which has the potential of having a major impact on your career.

Let us go through a few simple and easy-to-follow tips to make you look more professional.

Power Dressing for the Modern Man

While there is a lot of information out there on power dressing for the modern man, what I want to present in this book is an Indian perspective that will help young Indian professionals. There are a very few articles or magazines for the Indian man to help him achieve a professional look while retaining a unique Indianness in his dressing.

After exploring and researching on this genre, I have come across a power dresser—a young Indian who is not just stylish and dapper, but also understands that fashion and personality are meant to create magic if they match.

Jeremy Cabral is the name—when you talk about power dressing for Indian men, his name shines at the top of the list because he creates magic when he infuses fashion with his Indian personality.

He ventured into the world of fashion blogging with one purpose, and that is to 'share simple and easy-to-follow style guides for the modern Indian man'. This mantra has earned him a dedicated niche follower base across all social media platforms. Many young students are following him to understand 'power dressing', keeping in mind Indian culture.

Today, his fashion magazine *Fashion Most Wanted* has worked with some of the most premium brands in the country. In fact, he is the only Indian male fashion blogger to take up blogging as a full-time career. Needless to say, his style is classic and comfortable.

So, when you look at these pictures, you must be wondering if these attires are internationally accepted. The answer to this question is a big 'Yes'.

You should also not be surprised to know that the Nehru jacket is acceptable globally.

Power dressing looks by Jeremy Cabral
Photo courtesy: Sushant Sawant

Choosing Colours

In power dressing, a professional should remember that colours often have a greater impact than the outfit itself. The simple rule that most professionals follow is to go with deep, rich colours, such as blue, black, navy, charcoal and grey. While grey is conservative and sophisticated, black is undoubtedly the colour of choice since long. However, experimenting with colours is a new trend and brown is now gaining a lot of popularity in the professional space.

Focus on the Fit

A point to note is that no matter how great your outfit is, and even if the colour is great, if you wear an ill-fitting suit, it will make you look ungainly. Always focus on the fit. A simple test is to make sure that shoulders of the suit hug your shoulders. So, size it correctly to get the complete professional look, and let your suit do the talking.

Shoe Shopping

'We can tell a lot about a man by looking at his shoes.' These words are just as true in case of the business world. Let us go over the basics here.

- A black suit goes with black shoes
- A beige suit with brown shoes
- A brown suit with oxblood shoes will look amazing
- A grey suit with black shoes
- A navy suit with black or brown shoes

Though footwear is important, it is also important to take note of your socks. If you want to keep it simple, always match the socks with your trousers. While wearing a suit, you can also match your socks with your tie and pocket square[1].

While buying a pair of socks, remember to opt for cotton socks as they are better at allowing your feet to breathe. Also, never land up at your professional space in a pair of white socks. Save those for the sports day!

Pocket square
Photo courtesy: pexels.com

---

[1]The pocket square is something to flaunt, and it belongs in your jacket breast pocket. It is normally made of silk, light-weight cotton or linen.

Adding Accessories

Accessorizing is just as important as wearing the suit itself. A man's suit is incomplete without a tie, so choose your accessory carefully. The tie should highlight and not distract from your overall look. A silk tie with a conservative pattern, like stripes or a micro-grid, is appropriate for a business suit. However, bright colours such as yellow are fast gaining popularity. But do keep in mind the event you are going to, and I would personally recommend a conservative choice for a boardroom meeting. Keep the bright colours for your daily office look if you wish to flaunt your personality.

Let me once again emphasize on pocket squares as they are meant to add colour and personality to your suit. I recommend pocket squares and in matching sets for a clean, put-together appearance. Though it is not mandatory for your pocket square and tie to always match, they shouldn't clash either.

You can also go ties in for a tie clip—it is a functional and fashionable accessory that completes your look. When I say functional, I mean it is helpful to keep your tie secure and wrinkle-free throughout the day.

What about the wrist mate? Remember, a watch is your best mate, and even though we carry our cell phones with us at all times, most of us like to flaunt our watches. For a business suit, opt for a stainless steel watch with a blue or grey face to accent the colours in your suit and tie. For an Indian touch to your outfit, wear one with pearls or diamonds on the dial.

King Edward's Code

Let's talk about an interesting power dressing code for men: King Edward's Code.

We should be thankful to King Edward for bringing in this trend (or should I say confusion!). 'Sometimes, always, never' is the rule that all gentlemen need to know when they are wearing a three-button blazer—the middle button should always be fastened. The top button is up to you. But, what about buttoning the bottom button?

Don't even think about it!

You must be wondering how this rule originated.

Over a century ago, there were no hard-and-fast guidelines for buttoning blazers as some jackets had five or more buttons, and it was okay to fasten any number of buttons as per your choice. But all that changed in the late nineteenth century when England's King Edward VII, then the Prince of Wales, started growing a belly.

Edward liked to eat a lot of food. A lot! And it showed on his 48-inch waist, which grew faster than one would imagine! A time soon came when he could no longer fasten the last button of his waistcoat. Deciding that he liked the look, he kept it unbuttoned.

In an age when people were heavily influenced by royals, King Edward's practice of not buttoning the bottom button of his blazer gained popularity. Though the rule has illogical origins, over the years it became fashionable, and accepted as part of a professional dress code.

All the handsome gentlemen out there, do remember the 'Sometimes, Always, Never' rule.

Other Key Pointers

- Your clothes should reflect your personality, but remember power dressing is also a representation of your company, your industry and work environment. You are the brand ambassador of this image, so understand your responsibility.
- Take care of your personal hygiene from head to toe.

Remember to trim those nails and apply lotion on your hands and feet.
- Never wear strong perfume or cologne. Instead, choose a mild and pleasant fragrance.
- Wear well-kept and polished shoes.

Power Dressing for the Modern Woman

The first name that comes to my mind when I think of modern Indian women on the international platform is none other than Indra Nooyi, CEO, PepsiCo. She is truly a global citizen.

Ranked among the top 100 most powerful women in the world, her keen sense of dressing coupled with her persona make her a star that inspires women across the globe.

College Girl to a Classy Lady

As a young college girl, you need to transform yourself into a classy lady when you step into the professional world. This does not mean you stop living your life and having fun, but it is essential to ensure that you carry yourself as a 'professional' — not as a 'girl' or a 'woman entrepreneur' because talent has no gender.

So, what is the most attractive thing about you?

Having worked in the corporate arena, I can say without any doubt that nothing is more attractive than a lady with confidence.

There are a few key things that all youngsters can imbibe as they prepare to enter the corporate arena.

Dress for Success

1. Always take time out to look professional. It is not about expensive clothes and brands; rather, it is about wearing ironed clothes that are neat and clean and smell nice.

2. People first notice your clothes, so whether you like it or not, it is a good idea to invest some time in shopping for good quality clothes and ensure that they fit you well. It is imperative that you feel comfortable in the clothes you wear since you need to carry on in your professional attire for long hours. If your work involves frequent travelling, look out for wrinkle-free clothes. Plan according to your needs.

3. Women can opt for Western clothes or Indian, depending on the office culture. Although the 'salwar kameez' is not an acceptable choice of outfit in the international platform, most Indian women find it to be a comfortable choice, and so it is accepted as workwear in India. A tip is to wear bright-coloured stoles with cotton kurtas to complete the look.

   If I am wearing an Indian attire to my training workshops, I like wearing simple cotton kurtas with a deep, rich-coloured scarf. You too can get creative with your scarves and flaunt them as you please.

   So get the basics right; whether it is Indian clothes or Western, do complete your look.

4. Flaunt your Indianness at international platforms. Many people are surprised to learn that the saree is an internationally accepted formalwear. So, if you can carry it well and if you are comfortable in a sari, go for it! But remember to keep it simple; don't wear it in a flamboyant Bollywood style!

   The best part about sarees is its versatility. When choosing style, fabric and colours, opt for a more formal look. Choose colours like greys, yellows and pastels, and team them with high-neck blouses and keep them simple. If you are going for a conference, meet or an event, you may also add a jacket or a blazer. You will be surprised to see the transformation. Avoid floral prints and if possible wear saris without patterns.

Also, go for high-quality and genuine fabrics such as handloom, silk and bhagalpuris. Quality always shows, so don't stop yourself from spending a little extra for a fabric that will last.

Choosing Footwear

Always wear closed toe shoes like pumps; however, make sure you do not wear high heels. A heel height of 1.5–2 inches is appropriate and it keeps you comfortable on a long day. Flats don't go well with power dressing, just like high heels. The colour of footwear should be black, white, beige or burgundy (deep dark red); however, even brown works well, depending on your outfit. With a sari, you can always wear peep toes or sandals to take a break from closed toe shoes or pumps.

Adding Accessories

For power dressing, simple and minimal is the key — be it your watch or handbag.

Make sure your accessories are of good quality and brand, and avoid flaunting jewellery. Stick to the essentials. A silver chain with a small pendant will do, and if one can afford it, diamond is ideal. If you wish to wear gold, remember to keep it simple. A very thin chain is appropriate with a pair of ear studs and a watch — a slim silver one or a steel watch with a leather strap will do.

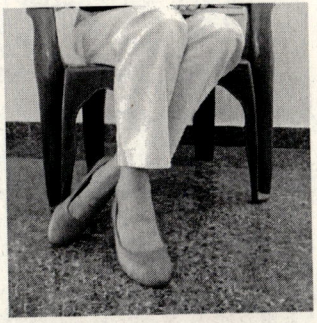

Photo: Anu Manhotra

For a sophisticated look that can be flaunted at big events, one can always rely on pearls. It is easy to get an elegant look by adding affordable white pearls, an ideal addition to Western and Indian outfits. Be it a saree or a blazer, you can always complete your look with pearls.

Carry a handbag, and if possible, match it with your shoes. Universal, classy browns and beiges are great choices, so is a rich deep-blue colour.

Doing Your Hair

There is one simple rule: Always tie your hair neatly in a bun. If you have long hair, tie it neatly in a French knot or chignon; if short, you can leave it open or use a small clutcher or make a high ponytail. Avoid bright and weird colour streaks on your hair, and manage your hair well, without needing to always brush it back.

Other Key Pointers

- *Arriving and leaving on time:* Ladies, do not give the excuse of having to play many roles back home and take the liberty to come late and leave early. Since we demand equality—and we deserve to be equal—we must accept our responsibilities too.
- *Internal strength:* As a professional, the best way to deal with hurdles, problems and difficult situations is to stay calm. Always remember to gather yourself and never let any external factor disturb your internal peace. You have to work on the art of always being in control.
- *Conversation:* Women are notoriously known for gossiping and talking a lot and not giving chance to others—mainly men—when in conversation. So, as

a professional, we need to understand the need to give equal weight to everyone in a discussion. Don't own the entire conversation—be a good listener and acknowledge others because this will give you room to learn and grow.
- *Don't be a mean girl:* Rather than gossiping or being mean to others, be a good critic and help others improve. Doing this, you will find that respect and love for others makes you a beautiful you.
- *Avoid being too good:* A lady will refrain from giving compliments that are not sincere. At the same time, avoid saying 'sorry' for small things. Statistics show that women tend to say 'sorry' a lot more than the word 'thank you'; so it shows that we need to work on this aspect of conversation. Be a confident lady.

Business Casuals for Women in India

What exactly is a business casual?

It is a style of clothing that is less formal than (formal) business attire; however, it still gives a professional and business-like impression when worn at the workplace.

Keep the workplace in mind and don't focus too much on the term 'casual' when choosing business casual outfits. Remember that even though casuals are allowed on weekends, it does not mean the type of casual clothes that you may wear at home.

Western business casuals for women mainly include slacks, khakis and chinos. A cowl neck top or a boat neck silk top would look great, so would neatly ironed cotton shirts. You can be creative with colours on weekends or daytime business events during weekends. Avoid wearing jeans and T-shirts.

My personal choice would be to pick something that is free-spirited and feminine. If you choose to wear an Indian outfit, a kurtas with palazzo or salwar kameez is a good choice. Avoid wearing leggings with long kurtas; instead, opt for a salwar or a trouser. Casual jackets are a great addition to business casual outfits. In winters, sweaters with varied patterns and colours can be worn. You can also carry your colourful handbag and wear accessories matching your attire. Open toe shoes and sandals make a good choice, but don't wear flats or flip flops even on weekends.

3

How to Promote Yourself

Self-promotion has nothing to do with ego. It is all about promoting a 'unique You'.

— Anu Manhotra

I always wonder why people do not promote themselves. Maybe it is because they don't ask themselves a question that I often ask myself: 'If I do not promote myself, then who will?'

So, embark on a fresh journey by asking these simple questions:

- Are we professionally promoting ourselves enough?
- Are we reaching out to everyone in the professional world without being obnoxious?

These are good questions to ask because there is a very high possibility that we are not engaging in adequate self-promotion. This is probably because most of us feel shy to talk about ourselves. Most of us are raised in a manner that views self-promotion as unthinkable and impolite.

However, in the contemporary corporate world, one needs to break these barriers and go all out with self-promotion because failing to do so will lead to nowhere.

Let us find out some great ways in which leaders promote themselves without sounding obnoxious.

Conducting and Participating in Events and Conferences

Actively participating in professional events such as independent talk shows for professionals (TED Talks, Talks at Google, 99u and Josh Talks) that are very popular all around the world will certainly help in self-promotion. This will ensure that your rich and useful contributions come into notice. Also, it helps that these platforms are not viewed as self-promotion platforms. Instead, people will encourage you to talk, promote and contribute more, as that will also help others to grow and gain from your expertise. So, a self-promotion idea that can also help others is a smart and sensible way to share your knowledge.

Best of all, when you get noticed you can also start organizing events and conferences where you can guide young leaders as well. They will not feel that you are going overboard to promote yourself because they will see you as an individual who is helping others in the professional arena.

Monthly Magazines

Yet another professional way to promote and talk in detail about your achievements, growth, learning and future plans is through monthly magazines. Numerous CEOs and companies use this strategy to provide literature not just to their employees but to all the stakeholders in the form of company magazines. These can be monthly or quarterly, and are a great means to reach out to many people in a manner that is dignified and in no way ostentatious or preachy.

Here, I would like to recommend the book *BRAG! The Art of Tooting Your Own Horn Without Blowing It* by Peggy Klaus, who is a top communications and leadership coach. This book suggests that simply working hard isn't enough to keep you shining bright as a professional; self-promotion is an important attribute for getting ahead.

Professional Networking Platforms

A true professional should not shy away from promoting himself/herself on the professional platform, as these platforms encourage only professional networking while prohibiting unnecessary exchange of personal information.

We are all familiar with LinkedIn, a site that helps you to create your professional profile. It is a platform where you can get recommendations from your colleagues, peers and managers. All these add to the value of your profile, and as a professional, you should request your connections to write recommendations for you. You should also make efforts to make the best use of this site by updating your profile regularly because this will help you promote yourself better, and also get noticed by those who matter.

Also, on these sites, professionals are noticed not for their personality, rather for their skills and quality of work. So, remember to keep promoting yourself on these professional platforms.

Self-Promotion for the To-Be Professionals

When talking about creating an image for ourselves to be presented to our 'potential employer', what comes to mind?

Yes, you guessed it right—a resume.

Whether we feel the need to look out for a new job or a more challenging position, the very first thing we start working on is our resume.

A resume is that piece of paper that reaches so many people—even before we get to meet them—and it conveys a great deal about ourselves. It reflects our educational qualifications, whether or not we have experience in a professional field, as well as a few necessary personal and contact details. Sometimes it even conveys our interests and strengths.

But is it able to present my attitude, my personality, my X factor?

The answer is 'no'. So how can I present all these traits, which are not presented in my resume? The answer to this question is: Visume.

Resume versus Visume

I strongly believe the one thing that will change within a year or two is the way we reach out and connect with our prospective employers.

In the past, we relied a lot on resumes, and as an HR professional I have given much advice on how to market and present oneself on that piece of paper called 'resume'.

Many professionals are highly paid to conduct specialized workshops just to help young professionals get their resume right, but all of a sudden I am noticing no demands for these resume writers! Seeing it decline within a 15-year span tells us that technology is fast-changing, and we all need to match it to stay up to date.

I am a big fan of the 'visume' myself, and strongly believe that this format will help you stand out and present the real you—something far better than the written resume.

What is a video resume?

Visume, as it is popularly called, is a small video clipping created by a candidate and uploaded on certain websites. These websites work with companies and are closely in touch with their respective HR departments. Video resumes can also be directly forwarded to HR teams. But remember to keep the video simple and appropriate to the job profile you are applying for. Also, make sure to check out the specific requirements of the organization in question.

When compared to the traditional resume, a visume is a great tool that can be used to market yourself. And yes, we do have experts in this field as well; just the way there are professionals for the written resume, there are others who can help you create a perfect video resume.

Tips on creating a visume

- Keep it simple and short—not over 90–120 seconds.
- Wear professional attire while creating the video, and imagine that you are sitting with an HR professional. Give complete attention to your 'visual image', and remember that body language plays an important role.
- Keep the background and location simple and professional.
- Prepare and practise in advance. A simple and crisp script said with confidence can get you your dream job.
- Create not just one but a few videos for different kinds of companies. You can dress accordingly while creating these different videos.

What are the benefits of a visume?

- A video resume helps capture your attitude and personality far better than the traditional resume.
- A visume helps you to present your social skills; it also shows the potential employer that you are more in tune with the latest trends and technology.
- You get to speak and present what you think are your USPs. Since you are the creator of the video, you get a chance to talk about your strengths and your unique selling points, unlike at an interview with the HR, where you can only answer what is asked of you.

- It is very easy to create a video of a minute or two, and is not at all a tall order.
- Visume is the new norm. It is the best option that has taken a lead over the traditional paper resume.

Possible disadvantages of a visume

A few studies find that video resumes are actually unfair and discriminatory in nature. While it is wise to keep video resumes ready with you, it is also important to check with your prospective employer before mailing it to the HR team.

Also, for people who are camera conscious, visumes can seem quite challenging. If you fall in this category, you can rehearse and practise in front of the camera before creating the final video. Remember, it always pays to face your fears and overcome them.

Business Cards

How can we not talk about business cards when we are talking of promoting our unique image? I certainly invest a lot of time in ensuring that my cards are up to date and carry my image along with that of my company/profession.

Business cards create a strong and positive image. Your small business card can help you get big connections. However, please keep a few things in mind.

- Don't display too much eagerness to share your card, especially if in conversation with someone who is senior to you in terms of experience and knowledge. Wait until they ask, and if it doesn't happen, you may ask and then share your card with them.
- Always make a positive comment about a card when you receive it.
- Don't scribble things on your card before sharing it.

- Always give and receive cards with your right hand; it will make a big difference when doing business on international platforms. Many follow the Japanese style of exchanging cards with two hands. You may opt for any one style or the other, depending upon your comfort level.

The two styles are illustrated for reference.

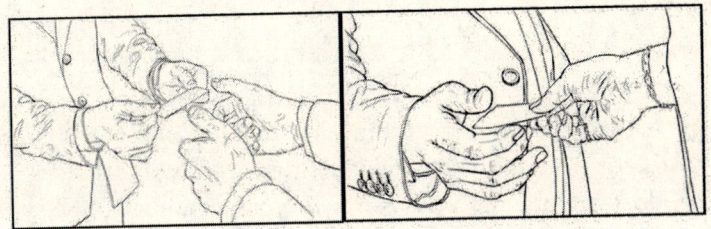

Illustrations by Vinai Mangalagiri

Website and Blogging

If you are a seasoned professional then you must certainly learn the craft of writing. Blogging rules the world today and gives deep insights on a variety of subjects. Hence, as a seasoned professional, the best way to promote yourself is through your professional blog or website, where you are able to present, share and discuss your work in detail.

In the contemporary world, there are unlimited tools to promote yourself, so leave no stone unturned and do not shy away from making the best use of resources available to market yourself without sounding arrogant. Get started on this journey and seize the opportunity to shine brighter.

4

How to Communicate at Work

The art of communication is the language of leadership.
—James Humes

Communication, both verbal and non-verbal, is at the foundation of everything we do and say. As a student or a young professional, strong communication skills can do wonders and add wings to your confidence that will lead you to succeed in both your professional and personal lives. It will help you transform from being a valuable to an invaluable employee or individual.

It is also important to realize that the workplace or professional arena is not limited or confined to one location nowadays. For instance, if you are working in Mumbai in India, it doesn't mean that you can survive speaking only the regional language. We live in a global era—a world where only global citizens are accepted as winners.

In the workplace of today, we have a diverse workforce where our co-workers, peers, superiors and colleagues are from the world over. They may be from different backgrounds, ages, cultures and countries, but one is expected to communicate well to stay connected with all in the work arena.

I cannot stress enough on the importance of good communication. Having spent quite some time in the corporate world as an HR Head, I realized that more than any degree or certificate, corporates want their employees to be able to communicate effectively and aptly use technology to stay connected with internal customers, clients and stakeholders. In fact, it is not far-fetched to say that good communication skills will help you reach the top of the corporate world and carve a niche for yourself.

Good Talker versus Professional Communicator

I strongly believe that one can be a good talker as an individual but that does not always mean they can communicate effectively in the workplace. This is because a true professional adapts, learns and unlearns various ways to communicate effectively based on organizational culture and job profile.

Let us dive deep to understand some ways to communicate effectively at the workplace.

Listen Before You Talk

All elements are equally important when we talk about communication. However, it is seen that 'listening' does not get its due as it is always underestimated. But the truth is that the secret to mastering workplace communication is listening.

This is a rare quality that only leaders admire. If you are asked to name the person you appreciate the most, I am certain you will name the one who listens to you first, then acknowledges and guides you.

This is what any good leader at an organization does, because they believe in paying attention to every team member, and taking time out to acknowledge their ideas and appreciate their views and lastly put forth their own opinion.

Communication, according to leaders in the professional world, is all about active listening.

Well, when I say 'active listening', it means you are constantly engaged as you listen to the speaker and you acknowledge them.

This helps in avoiding confusion and in case of a problem, a good leader will probe to better understand the speaker. So, it can be said that active listening is a great tool to appreciate your team, to avoid any confusion and work smoothly.

Acknowledge

I can't stop stressing on the fact that acknowledgement is one big gap between speakers and listeners. Once we fill this gap and make it a habit to acknowledge while listening, life will become much easier for all at work and things will start to fall in place.

Let us understand what exactly is acknowledgement.

Simply put, 'acknowledging is a simple way to make others feel valid and valued'.

As the first duty of love is to listen, so does the true professional leader listen and acknowledge the speaker in order to show them that they are valued and are an integral part of the workplace.

Acknowledging is the simplest art one can master even without talking, because sometimes all it takes is a nod or a tilt of the head or a smile on your face.

As a corporate trainer who conducts large and small training sessions, the biggest appreciation for me is an acknowledgement from the audience. It is the same for boardrooms or corporate conferences across the world. So, to be a great communicator, learn to acknowledge.

There are a few simple ways to acknowledge. Using these methods, you can make a significant contribution even as you listen.

- Work on your gestures and when you listen, maintain eye contact
- Lean forward slightly while listening

- Smile
- In a face-to-face discussion, you can supplement these gestures with small acknowledging words like 'Ah ha', 'Okay', 'I understand', and so on. These small words and gestures will take you a long way in connecting with the speaker. They also help avoid any misunderstanding or communication gaps
- A true professional and a great communicator will actually infuse and imbue more energy to big gatherings and dull meetings at the workplace by using appropriate acknowledgement

Speak Slowly

The business world is already loaded with so many complexities and problems; don't let your pace of speech add more to it. In fact, it could do a lot of damage. Keep this simple yet useful tip in mind: when you are meeting and working with a diverse workforce, remember to speak slowly and clearly. Speaking slowly also requires conscious effort, as most of us are really fast with our words. You must work at reducing this pace because when you speak fast, clarity takes a backseat and people may think that it is your lack of confidence that is making you speak fast.

Many sources suggest that a fluent English speaker speaks at a rate of 110–140 words per minute (WPM). It is a good idea to test your WPM rate and in case you are very far ahead of this range, you will need to practice speaking slower. Remember that speaking fast does not aid communication.

Know the Difference Between Language and Communication

Nobody can deny the importance of English, especially when we talk about it in relation to employment. Most MNCs and large organizations and educational institutes want their employees and students to communicate effectively in English. Not being able to speak in English can be a roadblock to success.

However, there is a lot of difference between the terms 'communication' and 'language' even though they are often used interchangeably. It is incorrect to use them as synonyms. So let us get down to brass tacks.

In simple words, communication is an art of presenting your ideas and thoughts in any language. In fact it possible to communicate without words, and ideas can be conveyed through body language, facial expressions or gestures. Communication is a very broad term whereas 'English' is a language and a skill. Remember, the more you practice, the more you hone your English-speaking skills. Skill is that special quality that is absolutely in your control. When efforts meet knowledge, nothing and nobody can stop you—not even talented individuals!

While at work, communication is not just limited to conversations, meetings and discussions. It also embraces technology. Modern workplaces function (and compete with each other) at very high speeds. Hence, one should not just acquaint and adapt to the latest technology at work but also use it at the right time and place.

This is important because sometimes overuse of technology can ruin and damage the human connect, and this is something rampant in workplaces where colleagues are often divided by and restricted to their cubicles. I have seen many employees who, despite constantly communicating with everyone at the workplace, are in reality totally disconnected.

For instance, email is a wonderful means to communicate quickly and in detail. However, we tend to forget that though it is very helpful when we need to communicate with people who are geographically distant from us, there is nothing like face-to-face communication. No form of communication can stir those emotions that a face-to-face conversation can elicit, so when faced with a choice of speaking to someone personally — for example a colleague in your office — it is best to walk over for a quick chat. This can always be recorded over a confirmatory email later on. Sadly, most millennials choose to email rather than having a face-to-face conversation.

So, we need to keep in mind that we communicate not just to share our ideas and thoughts but to connect with the listener or the audience. When you fail to understand this human element of 'connection', you limit communication to just a delivery of a message. To stay ahead in the professional arena, you must work on your craft of communication to ensure that you 'connect' with those you are speaking with.

5

How to Write Professional Emails

> *Reaching the inbox isn't your goal – engaging people is.*
>
> —Matt Blumberg

Are you:

- conscientious,
- intelligent,
- a subject-matter expert, and
- trustworthy?

Emails have a much greater impact than we imagine. It takes but one email to decode many things about an individual. So it is very essential that as a young professional, you must master the craft of email writing.

Let us discuss what is appropriate and what is not, when it comes to email etiquette.

Before I give you some great email-writing tips, let me ask, how would you like a companion who will always check everything you write? As an author, I always feel that I would like someone standing next to me and correcting whatever I write!

And I found a great friend in Grammarly! This is a software that will ensure that everything you write is clear, effective and error-free.

Let us now go over the main components of an email that make it a perfect piece of professional writing.

1. Subject line
2. Salutation
3. Body of the email (main content/reason for writing the email)
   - Formatting and font
   - Tone
4. Attachment
5. Sign off and signature

Subject Line

- A subject line is like a book title. This will give an idea about the story.
- So make sure to keep it flawless and KISS (Keep It Simple and Short).
- It should clearly express what the topic of the email is; however, ensure you don't reveal the details as it might have less chances of being read. Keep that suspense alive.

Common Errors

- Writing the subject line in all caps to convey urgency is considered unprofessional.
- Too catchy a subject is considered unprofessional. Instead, keep it smart and remember you are talking business here so follow decorum. Keep it 'catchy' and 'professional' at the same time.
- Avoid exclamation marks, except when you use phrases such as Register Now! or You're invited!

Sample Subject Line

- The promotion policy draft we discussed
- Follow up re: Training Schedule

- Thanks
- Special thanks from our Director
- Event Tomorrow. Register Today!

Salutation

In simple words, a salutation is a greeting.

Just as we say 'Hello' on meeting friends, a salutation is a greeting we use at the beginning of an email. As we all know, the most common form of salutation is 'Dear' followed by the recipient's given name or title. An appropriate greeting or salutation is extremely important as it sets the tone for your email communication, and is an indicator of your writing skills.

However, before thinking of a salutation, it is necessary to think about how well you know the recipient of your email. This is because we choose salutations based on how close our relationship with the recipient is—it could be a very formal relationship or it may be that you are writing to someone you have known professionally or personally for many years. In case of the latter, it is alright to use their first name. In case of the former, it is wise to use Mr or Ms followed by their complete name or last name.

Examples of formal email greetings:

- Dear [first name]
- Dear Mr/Ms [last name]

In case you do not know the names, you may try:

- Dear Sir or Madam

But try to find out the name because this makes your email a lot more personal.

Where you don't know a person's name or title, it's okay to use:

- To whom it may concern

But this salutation is very business-like without any personal touch.

Body of the Email

This is the main part of an email that reveals the reason behind your email. Hence, it is very necessary to know your audience before designing your content.

Let us discuss the '3 Point Rule', which is essential for effective email writing.

1. Write in paragraphs; don't merge the entire information into a long essay
2. For longer emails and complex information, use a bulleted or numbered list
3. Discuss only one main idea in the email

Also remember, it is crucial that the body of the email and the subject line go hand in hand. This is because the subject line (as mentioned previously) is like the title of a book, whereas the body text of the email is the story. Therefore, a connection between the two should be strong. In other words, the body of the email should be in sync with the subject line.

Formatting and font

- Black is beautiful in the professional world
- Always use the standard fonts such as Arial, Verdana, Calibri and Times New Roman
- Select a 10–12-point font size. In a long email, 10 point is ideal, and if it is just a few lines, 12 point is the best font size
- Avoid boldface and italics
- Avoid unnecessary styling of text because many users

set their preference to plain text as opposed to rich text. It might be a waste of time to put in effort to stylize your email, but in the end, the recipient only receives plain text—or worse, an email littered with alien characters
- Remember, using all caps is rude. In the cyber world, all caps is akin to SHOUTING!

Tone

Remember, 'emails = emotion'.

This means that people tend to remember the emotional tone of your email, even if they don't remember the exact words. The tone of your email also reflects your mood and personality. So, be very careful, because the reader will perceive your message in accordance with what they presume is your mood and personality.

The following elements convey the tone of your email.

- *Choice of words:* Keep your choice of words simple and professional.
- *Grammar:* Using full sentences and correct grammar are an important part of email etiquette. Incorrect usage of language diminishes the point of your email, and makes you appear unconcerned or uneducated.
- *Letter case:* Avoid using all caps and italics in the body or subject line of your email. It is considered rude.

Tips to convey professional tone

1. Never rush your email. Many emails come across as rude because we are in a rush and just want to get to the point. Sometimes a brief clarification may help. Even an exclamation mark can work to soften your tone. See the difference in the tone of the two examples below.

> Send the report by evening.
>
> OR
>
> Please send the report by evening as tomorrow new CEO is arriving, will appreciate your cooperation!

2. Always recheck before hitting the Send button. I remember my father used to correct me and tell me how important this small habit is—not only for emails but any piece of writing. Remember that this piece of writing also carries your personality.

   Make it a habit to review your email for content, spelling and grammatical errors because it does not give a good impression to your reader if your email contains typos.

3. Use polite words. We tend to ignore simple manners and forget the importance of 'respect'. Make sure to use common courtesy words such as 'Please', 'Sorry', and 'Thank you'. These words make your email sound respectful. For example:

   > Send me a copy of it.
   >
   > OR
   >
   > Please do send me a copy of it.

4. Never write an email when you are upset or angry. Remember that once an email is sent, it cannot be retrieved. When writing an angry email, consider the consequences not only for you but also for the intended recipient.
   If you must write an angry email, write it as a draft, wait overnight and revisit it in the morning. Then take a decision on whether to send the message or not.

An email case study

Here is an email from Amy to Zanny.

I can't tell you how much work is left for the meeting

tomorrow. You really need to be fast with your reports and presentations otherwise we will not be able to finish the work on time!

In this example, there is no greeting, only a demand that almost certainly would lead to a negative reaction. Had Amy rephrased her email and used correct email etiquette, it might have accomplished more.

Dear Zanny,

Thank you for your assistance today with the files. Also as the meeting is coming up tomorrow hope we are ready with the reports and presentation and do let me know if you need any help as we can together finish the work on time.

Kind regards,

Amy

Attachment

It is so easy to send an attachment, isn't it? But remember to consider the following points:

- *Size of the attachment:* Be very clear about the size of the file you are sending as an attachment—take the time to determine the file size. Anything over 500K (500,000 bytes) should be compressed or 'zipped' up.
- *Format:* PDF is the best bet; Word documents are generally considered unsafe as they can be easily modified by the recipient. Also, the best thing to do before sending the email is to ask the recipient what format he/she wants. This is to avoid sending files

- .they will not be able to open or access.
- *What to write*? Let us see some simple phrases we can use when we need to send an email with an attachment. For example:
  » Please find attached to this email a sample of...
  » Please find attached the list that gives the information you need.
  » As we discussed, I have attached the PDF showing...
  » The draft of my paper you requested is attached...

Sign Offs and Signature

- The last step is to include an appropriate closing with your name. 'Regards', 'Best regards', 'Sincerely', and 'Thank you' are all professional sign offs. Avoid ending your email with sign offs such as 'Take care', 'Best wishes' or 'Cheers', unless you are good friends with the reader.
- Your email signature allows your email recipient to quickly identify you — before even reading the email — and get in touch with you.
- Also, in order to stay up to date and not to have boring and bland signatures, add a few links in your email signature, including your Call to Action (CTA) and your social media icons.

Remember to send and reply to emails wisely, as they have the power to make or break a potential opportunity. I would like to end with a quote by Warren Buffet, 'It takes 20 years to build a reputation and 5 minutes to ruin it.' So think before you act, and in this case, before you hit the Send button!

6

How to Make and Attend Conference Calls

I hate it when I get ideas after a conference call!
— Anu Manhotra

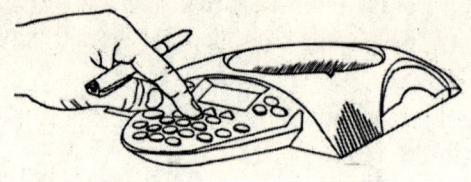

I used to be scared to even answer calls on my landline, and when I first saw this 'conference phone', I knew I was in big trouble!
Illustration by Vinai Mangalagiri

Basic etiquette in today's digital global era is no less than a dare; it is indeed a challenge, especially when you only have your vocal cords to rely upon.

During a conference call, you have only your voice to transmit your thoughts and questions. This can be pretty easy for someone who has great telephone and call etiquette but some of us dread to talk to complete strangers on the other side of the globe.

But, before we move ahead, understand your main concerns. List them down here.

1. _____
2. _____
3. _____
4. _____
5 _____

How to Attend a Conference Call

I must confess that I too used to be little scared of this device—the conference phone—as it looked so complex. It wasn't just the complexity of using the device but just the thought of speaking with so many people from around the world that gave me conference call anxiety! Let us now work together towards overcoming this fear of phones and conference calls. There are some guidelines you should follow when attending a conference call. Let us proceed in a step-by-step manner.

Understand the Device

It is very natural to be scared of something you do not understand or are not acquainted with. This applies to a new gadget or technology as well. If you spend just a few minutes to understand the technology in question—and in this case it is this conference phone and its buttons—it will soon become your best companion.

As a young professional, there will be many things that you will do for the first time, and it is understood that you will not know how to do them all by yourself; so, seek help from the IT department and ask them to explain to you how they work. In the case of conference calls, ask about the buttons that you need to use when making a call, how to dial, how to put someone on hold, and lastly, how to hang up.

It is always good to clear all your doubts regarding a new gadget than assuming that you will learn by observing others.

As a professional, you must be inquisitive and sure about the gadgets and the technology you will need to use in your daily work life. I was blessed to have wonderful leaders who always encouraged me to stay current and up to date. While you may not be as fortunate at all times, remember that inquisitiveness and confidence will take you a long way.

Always Come Prepared

It is essential to come prepared for a conference call as talking to more than one person at a time over phone can create confusion. It is best to be prepared with your queries and discussion points, and also to keep a pen and paper handy. If you are someone who likes taking notes on a tablet, keep it ready as well.

Speak Clearly

Speaking clearly is imperative as businesses today are no longer confined to a single state or country. We are living in a global world and are all global citizens. We need to meet and speak with people across the world on a daily basis, so differences in accents, cultures and languages are of great importance. Thus, the bottom line is to speak clearly and slowly when on phone.

Acknowledge the Speaker

One of the biggest confusions on any conference call is due to 'Dead Air'. During an in-person meeting, some quiet moments are easily understood because of our body language that negates the dead air. But this is missing in a conference call, and the silence can lead to confusion. So, the use of simple acknowledging words can be of big help. For example, 'Okay', 'Ah ha' and 'Let me think on it for a second'.

It is also important to keep talking, even when engaged

in an activity. For example, 'I'm just logging into my email now. Let me quickly search for your email. Here it is: "New project".'

By sharing these small details and sequence of events, you can tell the other participants that you are still actively engaged in the call.

Save Special Conversations for Offline

Let us suppose you're in a meeting with a group of 10 people, but you and another participant in the group are in discussion over a topic that holds worth only for the two of you. In such a situation, it is wise not to waste time of the eight other participants — save your discussion for after the conference call.

Remember time is money not just in a conference call, but everywhere. So make sure that because of 'your' important topic, you do not waste others' time.

If you know you have to discuss a particular topic with one of the participants, come prepared with a brief blurb on the matter, and then parlay the issue back to a later time. For example, you can suggest: 'Jim, let's take this offline.'

It Is a Wrap

When the conference call is coming to an end, it is always good to reach a consensus with all the other participants and summarize what was achieved during the meeting. This is to ensure that everyone is on the same page before signing off.

It is also necessary to have that one leader who will lead the call, introduce and connect, and the same person who will wrap up the conference call to avoid chaos and confusion.

Essential Vocabulary for a Conference Call

Address: This is to formally talk about something. For example,

'We need to address the recruitment problem today.'

Adjourn: This means to stop something until a later date. For example, 'Let us adjourn this issue for now and take up this matter next time.'

Any Other Business or AOB: This refers to an item on the agenda under which miscellaneous or random points are dealt with. For example, 'Well, as everything important is covered, Any Other Business, anyone?'

Hang up: Putting the phone down. It means to finish a call. For example, 'I'm going to hang up now as we have covered everything in today's agenda.'

Wrap up: This means to conclude, or to finish something successfully. For example, 'Brilliant, so to wrap up, we will have our next call coming Tuesday.'

Turn over: This means that it is someone else's turn to speak. For example, 'I will turn the conversation over to my colleague, Sam.'

7

How to Conduct a Meeting

When you go to meetings or auditions and you fail to prepare, prepare to fail. It is simple but true.
— Paula Abdul

Business and meetings are inseparable—we cannot grow, plan and expand our business until we have professional meetings. As a professional, you are either conducting or attending meetings, hence etiquette at these business meetings is very important. Adherence to proper etiquette for a business meeting ensures respect among meeting participants, helps the meeting begin and end on time and fosters an atmosphere of cooperation. A lack of etiquette and poor planning are two of the main reasons why many business meetings fail.

Let us look at the essential practices for planning and conducting business meetings like an expert.

Business Meeting Rules

Know what you want to accomplish: Write down the goals you want to accomplish in the meeting. Remember, it is necessary to have a valid reason for investing time in a meeting. When you have at least three valid points, it is good to call for a business meet. Refrain from disturbing everyone at work just to discuss one or two things. Three seems to be an ideal number, unless you have one or two very critical things to discuss. At the same time, it is not wise to have too many issues to discuss in a single meeting. This can lead to confusion and lack of clarity.

Familiarize yourself with the content of the meeting: It is always a good idea to come prepared to discuss what's on the agenda — this should be shared beforehand with all the participants attending the meeting. Working on the points mentioned on the agenda will ensure that you are an active contributor at the meeting and are a time-efficient resource.

Make sure you stay on topic: It is very easy to go with the flow, only to realize that the discussion has strayed beyond the agenda. Stick to the point to get the best out of the time invested in the meeting.

Participate and listen: Avoid being only a listener; every participant's views are mandatory. Be an active participant and present your views.

Body language (eye contact and bridging): While you listen to the other participants, make sure to have eye contact with the speaker and follow the bridging technique as discussed in Chapter 1.

Take notes: It is always good to prepare notes, as we cannot solely rely on our memory at all times. Most of us are mentally occupied all day long at our workplace, so these notes can come in very handy after the meeting.

Ground Rules

Every company has its own culture, and setting basic ground rules makes it convenient for everyone to understand the requirements of the company. In the same way, setting the ground rules for business meetings are also key to their success. For instance:

- » No meeting shall run over an hour. And if necessary, it can be continued after a short break.
- » Nobody is allowed to use their cell phones, so leave them at the workplace and carry Action Item lists for the meeting.

Other General Tips on Business Meetings

- Be mindful of your arrival time
- Take care of your attire for the meeting
- Create a summary of the points discussed
- Show off your best manners while disagreeing with someone
- Learn to endorse others' points of view
- Avoid nervous habits such as tapping a pen on the table, making noises with your mouth, rustling papers or tapping your feet on the floor

Helpful Business Meeting Phrases

As a professional, never shy away from improving your vocabulary on a particular subject. Many close friends of mine, who are at top levels at big organizations, still make sure they have crisp vocabulary on subjects like 'how to talk at business meets', 'powerful words to sound assertive', and so on. Believe me, it really helps. I would like to share some business meeting phrases that I learnt over the years working in the corporate world.

How to start a business meeting: This might seem very obvious that one needs to begin with a greeting and share the purpose of the meeting. But it is always a good idea to gather your thoughts *before* you step into the room, and even more so when you are chairing the meeting. For example:

- » Good morning/afternoon (and welcome) everyone.
- » The purpose of today's meeting is to discuss...
- » Thank you everyone for coming at such a short notice. Let's begin, shall we?
- » It's great to see everyone on time, so shall we start?
- » Now that everyone is here, let's get started.
- » Thank you for being on time, so without any further delay, let me introduce you [names of participants]...

How to introduce the agenda for the meeting:

- » I am sure everyone has a copy of the agenda?
- » Shall we take the points in the same order as mentioned in the agenda?
- » Let's look at the first item on the agenda.

Specifying the purpose/objective for the meeting:

- » We're here today to...
- » The purpose of this meeting is to...
- » The main objective is to...
- » I've called this meeting in order to...

Inviting others to speak: It is always good to invite others to present their views if you feel that a few of them are not opening up and sharing their ideas. As a chair, it is your responsibility to give this little push. You can encourage them by saying:

- » Would you like to open the discussion, Aarti?
- » What about you, Kaira?
- » What do you think about this, John?
- » What are your views on this, Rahul?

Sharing your point of view: Sometimes we tend to repeat words so often that people can guess what we are about to say. This can be an embarrassing thing and a sign that suggests your vocabulary needs some brushing up. Some ways to shuffle up things is by saying:
- I strongly believe…
- In my opinion…
- Obviously…
- As I see it…
- I believe…

Acknowledging the contribution of participants:
- You're absolutely right.
- True. Indeed!
- Exactly.
- Precisely.
- That's true, I suppose.
- I suppose so.

Disagreeing with others at the meeting:
- I don't really agree.
- I am sorry I don't agree.
- That's not really how it is in my opinion.
- I'm afraid I disagree with you there.
- Well, I don't know…

Advising and suggesting:
- How about…
- What about…
- I suggest…
- I recommend that…
- I believe we should…

Checking for clarity:
- » Sorry, I didn't get that.
- » Sorry I didn't catch that. Could you repeat that, please?
- » I missed that. Could you say it again, please?
- » Sorry [with proper intonation is also sufficient sometimes].

Ensuring the meeting ends on time:
- » I'm afraid we've run out of time.
- » That's not really why we're here today.
- » We'll have to leave that for another time.
- » Keep to the point, please.
- » We're beginning to lose sight of the main point.

How to summarize the key points of the meeting:
- » This is what we've all agreed on.
- » Before we wrap up, let me just summarize the main points.
- » In brief...
- » To sum up...

Thanking the participants for attending:
- » Thanks a lot for coming.
- » Thank you all for coming.
- » Thank you all for attending.
- » Thanks for your participation.

Relying on Case Studies: Activity Time

As an MBA student, I find the 'case study method' a very helpful style of learning. It is popularly used in many MBA courses and focuses on the student as a decision-maker. This method encourages the student to work independently without the intervention of an educator.

The following case study will reflect upon problems that

occur in business and will give you an understanding of the corporate world.

Effective meetings are essential, and we all agree that there is nothing worse than attending a non-productive meeting. Given your experience, what advice would you give to Lalit and Sudha?

Case Study 1

Lalit is a senior executive at a mid-sized company. His work team comprises sales and operation vice-presidents and directors. Lalit is, by nature, an introvert. He is an excellent processor of data and has proven himself throughout his years at the company with his ability to get the job done. At his team meetings, there is always a lot of discussion. Recently, he notices that team members are arriving late, leaving mid-way, and can be seen multitasking on their Blackberries during the meetings. Week after week, meetings are dragging on without much of anything getting accomplished. What can Lalit do next to get his meetings back to being effective?

Case Study 2

Sudha has just been promoted to a team manager position. She has been very successful as an engineer. She is now about to hold her first team meeting and many of her team members are colleagues that she worked with side-by-side for the past two years. What advice would you provide to Sudha in order to have an effective meeting?

Answers

Lalit must come out of his shell and build his interpersonal skills. He should be more confident and assertive in sharing his ideas. Lalit must follow the 3 Objective Rule.
He should set ground rules.

He should see to it that all participants are contributing.

Sudha should start with setting ground rules.

As team members know her very well, she should assign responsibilities and roles very clearly before the meeting.

Simple techniques such as power seating can be employed to stay in charge.

8

How to Handle Lunch or Dinner Meetings

Dining is an art and you can't master it without having great taste for it.

— Anu Manhotra

Ways to Ace a Business Meal

Since the craft of connecting in the business world is very crucial, why not do it over a business meal?

If given a chance to meet your client or a new business contact over a meal, far away from boardrooms and the clutches of technology, would you be up for this opportunity?

Or, do you feel that you lack the confidence to do this?

If your answer is in the affirmative, don't worry or lose sleep over it because a set of key rules will help you show up with confidence at any business meal — be it a power breakfast, brunch, office party or a classic 17-course French meal. You will be able to ace them all!

Bring Them On

I am talking about bringing your manners along with you at the table. Always be courteous to the waiting staff; do not complain or criticize the food or service.

Arrival

As a host, ensure that you are arriving early on the day of the meeting so that you can secure the best table and greet your guest/s on arrival. Do not forget the firm handshake. If possible, sign the receipt in advance and include a tip for the waiting staff.

Purse and Briefcase

Having arrived, now the question is: where does the purse/handbag or briefcase go? The answer is simple; it goes on the floor, close to your chair. Do not keep it in the way of passage, and ladies, do not hang it on the chair or place it behind you. It *must* be placed on the floor.

Digital Companion

Your cell phone is probably your most constant companion without which life is unimaginable. However, when at a business meal, it is highly recommended that you switch off your cell phone, and also ensure that it is not placed on the table.

We Are Equal

Remember, this is a business setting and you need to leave gender aside. Do not pull out a chair for a lady—she can do it for herself.

Be a Guest

If you are a guest, be a good one at that and follow the host. This means that while dining, be patient and let the host first settle down. Let them first place the napkin or start eating before you do the same.

Napkin

When you are seated, take your napkin and place it on your lap. However, if you are attending a very formal gathering, where there is a definite host or hostess, wait for them to place their napkins on their laps first before you do the same. Simply unfold it, but do this quietly with your hands under the table. Remember it is a napkin and not a tissue.

Once you've placed it on your lap, the napkin should not touch the table surface again, until you have finished your meal. If at any point you want to be excused for some reason in the middle of the meal, you can do so by placing your napkin on the chair.

Inedible Food

Never spit into your napkin, even if you find something on your plate inedible.

Be careful when you place an order for a meal; however, in case you have ordered something that you find inedible or worse find it in your mouth in the middle of a conversation, excuse yourself from the table. You can visit the restroom for a quick fix. Else, you could use your thumb and index finger to remove the morsel from your mouth and then wipe your fingers on the napkin.

BMW Rule

This is a wonderful mnemonic that helped me and I am sure it will help you too.

BMW in dining etiquette stands for 'bread, meal and water'. Remember that your bread-and-butter plate is on the left, the main meal is in the middle and your water glass is on the right.

Complex Cutlery

Most of us do not have experience with specialized cutlery—it is neither taught in school nor used at home. But it is never too late to learn and with practice, it might become second nature. So, let's dive right into the world of silverware.

Two simple rules here: one, start on the outside and work your way in and, two, forks on to the left of the plate, and knives and spoons to the right.

Another thing to remember is that most of the time, cutlery above the plate includes the dessert fork and spoon, though these may occasionally be placed parallel or diagonal to the plate.

Finger Food

Bread is finger food, so tear small pieces with your fingers and butter them with your butter knife as you go. Do not eat an entire piece of bread at one go, and do not butter a whole slice of bread at one time. If the butter is located on a central dish, take a portion of it and place it on your bread plate.

À La Carte

It is always good to opt for food that is easy to eat. At times, a regular buffet or set meal can be messy to eat. At such instances, an à la carte menu is ideal, where you can order individual items as per your choice and comfort.

Discussing Business

A business meal doesn't mean that as soon as you sit down, you start talking business. Respect the social setting and begin with a social conversation with your guest after you have been seated; wait until your beverages and the first course is served and eaten, then start talking work.

Full Course Dinner

A full-course dinner consists of multiple dishes/courses. In this context, a 'course' refers to a specific set of food items that are served together during a meal.

A popular and an economical choice in India is the three-course meal. This meal includes a standard sequence with appetizers, the main course and finally, dessert or a hot beverage such as tea or coffee.

Like the three-course meal, there is also the four-course meal that includes an appetizer to start the course followed by soup/salad, main course and dessert.

A five-course meal includes five components: soup, appetizers, salad, the main course and dessert.

The Legendary 17-Course French Menu

A 17-course menu might sound very extreme, but know that this is often spread across a long evening—often four to five hours—and the courses that are offered are in small quantities. This type of meal is generally served at very formal events.

Let us dive into this extravagant food love story.

Starters

1. *Hors d'oeuvre:* This is the French for appetizer (pronounced as 'hordervs'), and is very popular at restaurants these days. These are served on rotating trolleys or offered on trays by the waiting staff.
2. *Soup:* Both thick, creamy soups (known as potage in French) and clear soups are offered.
3. *Oeuf:* The French word for egg is oeuf. This course includes dishes made with eggs as the primary ingredient.
4. *Farineaux:* A variety of rice and pasta dishes, such as spaghetti,

lasagna and gnocchi are offered as part of this course.

Main Course

5. *Poisson:* Don't be scared of the name! These are the dishes prepared with fish.
6. *Entrée:* A small dish served before the main course.

At this point, there is a small break between the courses.

7. *Sorbet:* This is a frozen dessert, similar to the Arabian sherbet.
8. *Releve:* This the main meat course on the menu. Releves are the large joints of meat that are typically roasted. This course is always served with potatoes and vegetables.
9. *Roti:* This means roast. It includes poultry chicken, turkey, duck or pheasant.
10. *Legumes:* This course contains dishes prepared using vegetables.
11. *Salad:* Various types of salads are served during this course.
12. *Cold buffet:* In this course, small pieces of chilled meats are served.

Afters

13. *Entremets:* They refer to desserts, and can include hot or cold sweets, gateaux, soufflés or ice cream.
14. *Savoureux:* This is a savoury dish and includes fried bread or toast with a spicy filling inside. So if you are someone who does not have a sweet tooth, you can go for a savoureux at the end of the meal.
15. *Fromage:* All type of cheese may be offered in this course along with suitable accompaniments. The ideal cheese board will be a combination of hard, semi-hard, soft or cream, blue and fresh cheese.

16. *Dessert:* This course includes cut fruits, nuts and other common desserts such as cakes and candies.
17. *Boisson:* A hot or cold beverage is served to finish the meal.

As a professional, deep knowledge of French haute cuisine is not needed. However, the 17-course French menu is a legendary course and some basic knowledge of it will do no harm.

Hot Beverages

Tea and coffee are the real delights of life, and there are tea and coffee lovers all over the world. Let us go over a few pointers for drinking them right.

- Use big mugs for coffee
- Small cups are for tea
- On the table, the bigger and leaner pot is for coffee
- The teapot is generally smaller and stouter in shape
- Avoid leaning forward to sip on your tea. Instead, bring the cup to your mouth and leave the saucer on the table itself
- While adding sweetener or sugar, tear the sachet gently and do not scrunch up the package. Leave the empty sachet on the saucer. If adding sugar cubes, do not stir your beverage by swirling the spoon; just go back and forth slowly without making a clinking sound
- For the ladies, hold the cup firmly and do not let your little finger stick out as you sip from the cup
- Tea may also be a great way to network. This can be an afternoon tea or even high tea, which usually takes place late in the evenings. A high tea includes snacks. If one needs to learn the ABCs of etiquette for tea drinking, learn it the British way.

Learning About Cutlery Positions

Continental-style Close-out Position

The continental dining style close-out position is the most popular and easiest dining style to master. To follow this style, place the fork (tines down) and knife diagonally on the plate at a 4 o'clock position.

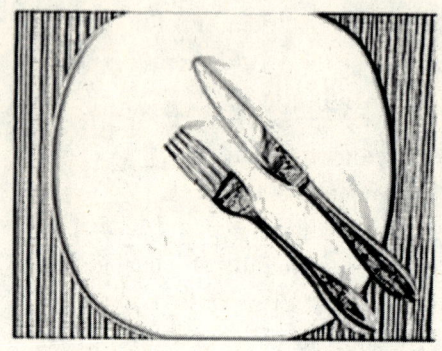

Fork and knife rest and close position
Illustration by Vinai Mangalagiri

Resting Position Continental Dining Style

If you want to pause or talk during the meal, place the cutlery in resting position on the plate to indicate your pause without saying it out to the waiting staff. All you need to remember is 'V'

Place your fork with tines down and knife in an upside down 'V' position as shown in the illustration.

Resting position continental dining style
Illustration by Vinai Mangalagiri

American Dining Style Close-out Position

This illustration demonstrates the American dining style close-out position. The only difference with the continental dining style is that the knife is on or close to the fork.

American-style close-out position
Illustration by Vinai Mangalagiri

American-style Resting Position

In the American dining style if you want to signal to the server that you are not yet finished with your meal, and you have just taken a break to sip water or wipe your mouth with a napkin, you can convey this without saying a word by following this illustration.

Simply place your knife at the top of your plate and always remember to keep the face of the blade (of the knife) inside and the fork in the 4 o'clock position, with tines up.

American-style resting position

Illustration by Vinai Mangalagiri

Other Miscellaneous Things to Remember

No Elbows

You have probably heard this many a time before that at a meal you must maintain good posture—do not slouch on the chair and no elbows on the table. This, however, does not mean that you should always keep your hands and wrist away—wrists on the table are acceptable and so are free arms.

Waiting staff

At a business meal, you can either make or break a deal depending on how you treat the waiting staff. Always be polite and kind to everyone who serves you. Remember this is the finest way to conduct yourself.

Handle with Care

Do not stack your dishes or push them away from you after your meal is complete. Wait patiently for the waiting staff to clear your items.

Handling the Bill

As the host, you pay—no confusion here at all.

It is a very simple rule: If you have invited guests, you must pay for the meal. Use proper etiquette in this regard and pay the bill ahead of time. To do this, speak with the manager of the restaurant, and provide them with your credit card information or give them your card. (Not in front of the guests, of course!) Also, remember to attach your business card and share your complete details such as your name, phone number and email address, so the final receipt can be mailed to you.

Tipping

Tip stands for 'To Insure Prompt Service' or 'To Insure Promptness'. In Indian restaurants that do not levy a service charge, a tip of around 8–10 per cent of the bill is considered respectable. However, in case there is a service charge—something akin to a compulsory tip that is already charged to the customer—it is acceptable to forego the tip.

Tips to Add Extra Finesse to Your Dining Experience

- This is a very personal tip but believe me it works! If you are going for a business meal, you typically have two things on your agenda—business and a meal, in that order. Giving more importance to business and less focus on the food is appreciated. It is wise to have something before your meeting so that you don't show up too hungry with only food on your mind! Having a light snack or fruit before leaving home is advisable.
- Appropriate attire is essential and there are two things to keep in mind here: restaurant and your business clients. Not only should you dress according to the type of business meeting you are attending, you should also do some research on the restaurant you will be going to.
- Remember to offer to the person on your left and pass everything to the right.
- If someone asks you to pass the salt at the table, always pass the salt and pepper together.
- When you are not eating, keep your hands on your lap or resting on the table (with wrists on the edge of the table).
- Do not slurp soup from a spoon. Always spoon the soup away from you when you take it out of the bowl and sip it from the side of the spoon. If your soup is hot, do not blow on it; rather, let it sit until it cools down.
- For business meals, always come prepared for well-informed small talk.
- No alcohol at a business meal.

9

How to Put Colleagues and Business Associates at Ease

Never forget the two most important elements in business — communication and connect.
—Anu Manhotra

On my first-ever business trip to Miami, USA, it was not just the cold weather that made me uncomfortable, it was also the lack of warmth in the behaviour of associates and managers at the manufacturing facility I had visited. At the time, I was representing my company, an aerospace firm, as an HR head. Though I felt bad, I took it as my share of learning and decided that I would never let myself or my team make any visitor or business associate feel the way I did.

This trip was a little hectic as I had to touch base at two manufacturing units in a short period of time. After my visit to Miami, I flew down to Tucson and I was surprised by the way I was welcomed and received by everyone, including managers and members at the facility. It made me realize that it is not the place or the geographical location that matters, it is in fact the culture of the organization that makes all the difference.

The major difference between the two manufacturing facilities I visited was the behaviour of my colleagues, managers and executives. At the Tucson facility I felt the warmth because

I saw a welcoming smile on everybody's face, and people took interest in acknowledging and giving a minute or two to get to know me and also understand my job profile. All this made me feel so much at ease.

Though I was confident and believed in open communication, I realized on this business trip that to be a global professional, only communication skills are not sufficient. What we all need along with communication skills is a sense of 'connect'—the human element, which makes us feel at ease. No matter which part of the world we work in, we all need to have a strong connect with our clients, customers, peers and colleagues.

When this connect is missing, you are not at your best—no matter what set of expertise you carry. You will not be able to enjoy your work or live your passion. You need to understand that it works the same way for the other party as well. For instance, a business associate will not be able to give their best to your company and team, if you are not able to make them feel comfortable. So the key learning here is that 'without connect, even communication will become a burden'.

Over the years, I have observed that in the business arena, sometimes we do not treat people as humans; rather, we treat them as 'titles'—we give them respect and communicate only to the point that is defined by their job roles. No less, no more, and this is where we all go wrong.

Be it a top-level executive or a novice at the office, we should remember to treat everyone with courtesy and this goes the same way with our business associates, clients and customers. It should not be limited to the employees of our organization.

Before this experience, I was just an HR Head in the company but after this short business trip, I transformed into a great 'team member'. This trip had a huge impact on me as a person and I say so because it made me free—free from titles and business tags. After this business trip, I did not feel the need for a title at all. What a transformation it was for me, and I found peace at being able to work without tags and title. The level of joy that I experienced in empowering myself and my team is beyond words. For this experience and transformation, I will be ever thankful to my boss who had decided to send me on this trip.

I hope and wish that all of you get the chance to travel a lot. I would like to share a few golden tips I picked up along the way. This will help you ensure that your colleagues and associates are working with you and your organization effortlessly and wholeheartedly.

Face of the office/facility

First things first, let us begin with this question: How much warmth does the reception of your office exude towards first-time clients, associates or customers?

Rate it on a scale of 1 to 5, with 5 being the highest score. This is a simple activity one can try before a new client is scheduled to visit the facility. Since the reception area is the face of the office, it needs to be welcoming. Very often, we tend to forget the physical aspect of the entire setting, especially the reception area, so keep in mind that this tangible element should be given due importance. Such things should not be ignored. Let us go over some easy tips to add more warmth to this area.

1. A personal welcome message on the noticeboard or on a wall at the reception will surely bring a smile to the new visitor's face. It makes for a good start to any conversation. It can be something as simple as 'Welcome Josh, Team XYZ'.

2. It is mandatory for the organization to train all top-level executives on how to treat their internal and external customers. These managers will then pass on their learnings to their team members, so that they are equipped with the necessary training to make a positive impact on business associates and clients. It should not be that we ignore these small things and allow them to snowball into a big deal later on. Remember, it is better to be prepared than sorry.

Now, the question is: what should the training entail?

- It could be as simple as training every employee on meeting and greeting confidently. Sometimes it is embarrassing to find that when a very important business client is in the facility, employees feel nervous and are unable to introduce themselves with ease. Though it is the responsibility of the HR Department to train every employee, basic courtesy and greetings can always be learnt without anybody's assistance, and as a true professional one must learn to meet and greet business clients and associates.
- At times, there could also be a generic discussion to update all employees about the importance of a client's visit. Though the visit of a new client or business associate is not a confidential matter, it is something that is often not shared openly by many organizations. As a result, many in the facility are not aware of any visitors in the facility. This can lead to a negative impact when the associates are seen as strangers by a few employees. Thus it is mandatory to pass on the communication about the visit of any new associate or client.
- Training the support staff to coordinate properly with

a new employee, a client or a business associate is also essential.
- Giving detailed guidelines to the housekeeping staff is also mandatory.
- Anger management and sensitivity training workshops can be organized on a regular basis.

3. As I shared through my experience, it is often office culture—its vibe and warmth—that can make or break business deals and relationships. So, one must ensure that everyone in the company is contributing to strengthen this positive vibe.

All these aspects need to be embedded in the system from top to bottom—not by force or compulsion, but by showing employees and making them understand why it must be done.

Importance of Office Culture

1. One cannot stress enough on the importance of business ethics. As a true professional in the twenty-first century, we must not be ethically blind, though it is very easy for young professionals to get swayed early in their careers. However, when the company and its pacemakers clearly promote 'business ethics' over 'business gain', it provides a positive and healthy work environment where employees do not compete blindly but help each other grow. It also leads to a sense of mutual respect that helps the organization stay away from unnecessary clutter blocking its path to success.

2. The second most important thing I want to highlight is the importance of business etiquette. One of the easiest and most sought-after way to show respect to your colleagues (or clients) is through good etiquette. These unwritten rules come handy in any business situation, and help you

act professionally and respectfully.
3. The third rule is strict adherence to good manners and courtesy towards everyone in the organization. Before you learn business etiquette (and even when you are not sure about the correct etiquette), you can always rely upon our good manners and three magic words—'Please', 'Sorry' and 'Thank you'—to build a positive relationship with your business associates.
4. Group cohesiveness is another crucial factor for good office culture. All employees should work together as a big team and towards a common goal. When we work as true team members, forgetting our titles and tags and keeping aside our egos, work can be done more effectively.

What about Refreshments?

Have you ever faced a situation where you have travelled far to visit a facility and after reaching, heard these scary words: 'We are out of coffee today.' Or, 'The vending machine is in for repair. We are sorry.'

Horrible, isn't it?

Imagine you are that person who has travelled far, and then this happens to you.

Don't ever let this happen in your facility. If you know that you are going to have a visitor at your office, make proper arrangements and coordinate properly with other departments such as admin as well as housekeeping and support staff. This way you never cut a sorry figure in front of the visitor, and at the same time don't make them feel uninvited and unwanted.

You should also not hesitate to provide refreshments. It is the least one can do to make others feel welcome and comfortable.

Remember the Human Element

We often forget that business associates and new colleagues are humans like you and that they exist beyond their titles and business tags. Judging them or treating them as per their ranks comes across as very cold behaviour. Remember that respect is an intangible element that is expected of each one of us. It can never be demanded or asked for, but only gained when we show respect to others through our behaviour and words.

In a workplace this becomes more critical because we all have different ideas, opinions and ways of doing things; hence, conflict and disagreement is natural. However, when a workplace has a good culture, things become easier and conflicts are avoided through discussion.

Why Respect Is Important at the Workplace

1. To stay happy at the workplace, as we all yearn for respect and dignity
2. To stay away from office politics and stress
3. Exchange of ideas because healthy discussions take place
4. To get a more productive workforce
5. Avoid judging colleagues, clients and stakeholders. We all come from diverse organizations and so must learn to tolerate others' views and be patient

10

How to Build a Positive Corporate Culture

> *Customers will never love a company until the employees love it first.*
>
> —Simon Sinek
> Author, *Start With Why*

Corporate Culture

As a true professional, it is necessary to understand corporate or office culture of the workplace. Let us begin by answering a few simple questions.

Define culture or your office culture in your own words.

_____
_____
_____
_____
_____
_____

What kind of communication atmosphere does it provide?

_____
_____
_____
_____
_____
_____

Does your office regularly communicate or remind you of its vision and mission statements?

_____
_____
_____
_____
_____

Defining Culture

If I have to describe culture in one word, I would say culture is 'organic'.

I say organic because it is crafted by individuals such as you and I. The culture of an organization, home, school or any other group is crafted by us.

Culture is defined as the values, beliefs, underlying assumptions, attitudes and behaviours shared by a group of people. It is the behaviour that results when a group arrives at a set of—generally unspoken and unwritten—rules for working together.

This is good news for all of us as it gives *us* the power to recreate a culture and make it more positive, if we are not happy with the current culture at our college, home or workplace. Thus, we can say, 'culture is you and me'. Let us now invest some time to craft an inspiring and evolving culture in which people can come together to work happily without stress.

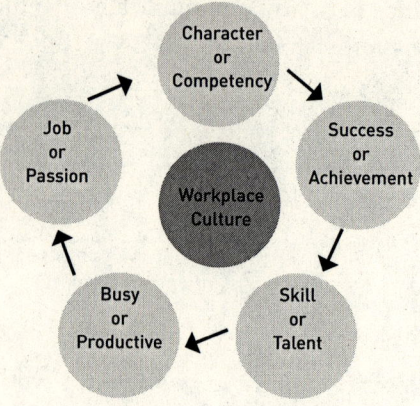

Elements of Culture
Graph by Anu Manhotra

Since we agree that culture is organic and that every employee contributes towards it and is responsible for creating the culture of the workplace, let us discuss the elements upon which we can craft a new organic culture.

Character or Competency

Organizations that only lay emphasis on competency of employees can become good organizations, but those that value both character and competency are the ones with a truly great culture. These organizations have at the core of their business, not just economic viability but also business ethics. They have a great culture that truly promotes and fosters not just competency but more importantly, happy professionals with strong morals. Hence, this culture promotes a healthy work environment and ultimately positive results.

So, organizations and employees should always strive to become great professionals and work honestly and ethically. An example of such an organization is Infosys where the character of an employee is given due credit in addition to encouraging healthy competition.

Success or Achievement

Many organizations promote the culture of success, which is not a bad thing in itself; however, if we look deeper, this type of culture can lead to other problems—a good employee can begin to doubt his/her ability, high competition to succeed may bring in fraudulent ways in the system, and so on. Unlike these organizations, there are few others that promote the culture of achievement.

But first let us understand the difference between the two terms, success and achievement.

Success in office culture is all about external appreciation, reward and recognition.

Achievement, on the other hand, is all about a 'sense of achievement'. It is celebration of each goal reached by the individual, irrespective of how big or small they may be. This motivates employees to keep growing, so no big event is needed to acknowledge their contributions. Of course, celebrations do take place, but they celebrate baby steps and the collective effort of the employees. So we can see how this type of culture promotes self-confidence and working without supervision. The competition is more within, that is it inspires every individual to compete with their previous achievements and grow better each day to meet their best self.

We all should know that such companies do exist, and the perfect example is perhaps no other than Google—an organization where employees are confident without the need for external motivation to give their best.

Skill or Talent

As discussed in Chapter 1, we now understand the difference between skill and talent.

Great companies understand the beauty of skill, so they encourage a culture of positivity and trust and give time to individuals to learn, practice and grow. They believe in the power of training and value every individual unlike those that believe that only 'talented' individuals should be hired. In the real world, the practice of hiring only talented individuals is actually impossible, and so corporates with this kind of culture—they do not believe in investing in training and encouraging employees—suffer high attrition rates.

As individuals, you must know that even if you are not good at something, if you keep working at it, over and over again, you can master the craft and become a productive employee for the organization.

Organizations that invest in training are highly successful because they are the sum total of what employees achieve individually. Therefore, organizations should do everything to ensure that employees perform at their peak and give their best. A good example of such an organization is Tata Consultancy Services (TCS). It is India's largest software exporter and invests a lot in upgrading the skills of its employees.

Busy or Productive

This is another very important element of office culture. It is especially relevant in the Indian context as we seem to thrive on a culture where working late or overtime is met will approval and encouragement. In such organizations, it is common to find seniors supporting employees who stay back in office even after completing eight hours of work. They often stretch their working hours to show everyone around that they are very busy, and consequently win praises from their seniors and managers.

However, this culture is extremely dangerous as it clearly shows that an employee is not able to get the work done in the required time; hence, productivity is low. We need to be very clear that being productive and time-effective is essential, and this should be promoted in every organization. The message should be that anybody can be busy, but if you are not productive, you are not a valuable resource for the organization. Hence office culture should promote productivity and ensure that all employees are able to finish their task in the given time, which will make them more productive rather than sluggish.

Just a Job or a Passion

Passion is an emotion that comes from within. It is your zeal and enthusiasm towards your work that will keep you, as well as others around you, happy. So, the question is: how many of us are happy doing the work we do?

At the workplace, a major reason behind not achieving optimum results is the lack of passion. We take work as a burden and don't love doing what we do.

If the organization has a culture where employees crib about their work, this will be passed on to newcomers as well. When this happens, work is equated with burden. On the other hand, in companies where employees love their jobs, their work is not just work to them; it is an expression of their creativity. Organizations with this kind of positive culture are the best places to work at because they foster creativity and respect for everyone—internal customer, external customer, top management and all employees. So, choose the profession that you can be passionate about, so that every stage of your work is a celebration rather than a burden.

According to *Fortune* magazine, Salesforce, which is an American cloud-based software company headquartered in San Francisco, California, is the happiest workplace in the world.

According to an employee at Salesforce:

> This is an extraordinary, special place that really cares about its employees, customers, and community alike. We are strongly encouraged to give back to the community. I have done everything from working in a soup kitchen to working in a children's hospital in Morocco—all supported by the company. We have many opportunities to do the best work of our careers, be recognized for it and advance. I feel I can be creative and offer solutions that really help the company be successful. Most importantly I look forward to coming to work every day, working with our wonderful community and doing satisfying challenging work.

FAQs

- How will you communicate with your internal customer? In order to answer this question, you need to ask yourself: what should be the culture of my organization? Should it be one that relies on gadgets or face-to-face conversations?

We've become so reliant on our digital companions that we've started to neglect the art of conversation. While technology is wonderful for improving speed, it can have a detrimental effect on personal relationships. How many times have you sent an email with the best intentions, only to have its message misconstrued at the other end? A short response sent in haste can easily be misinterpreted as lack of care—or worse, a sign of anger.

- How to handle cut-throat competition?

You can satisfy the need to bond by creating a corporate culture that is based on mutual respect and support. Instead of making employees compete against one another—this creates a cut-throat environment where employees willingly step over their co-workers to climb up the corporate ladder—reward employees as a team to encourage camaraderie. When you encourage them as a team, internal competition will fade away but not the zeal to stay ahead.

- How can you find your voice at the workplace?

As we are liberated from our own fears, our presence automatically liberates others. So are you liberating your team members or are you hiding inside the team?

An organization's culture should be open and communication is the key. Be open about your fears—voice your fears and learn to overcome them.

Cross-cultural Communication

Cross-cultural communication is that magic glue that bonds people from different cultures and languages together and fixes all problems.

In this section, we will look at a few tips and strategies that will help you identify possible cross-cultural issues and misunderstandings in communication and apply strategies to overcome these issues in a global setting.

Understanding Cross-cultural Communication

In simple words, cross-cultural communication refers to communication that takes place between people belonging to different cultural backgrounds. This is necessary as this helps create better understanding and coordination between individuals or teams, leaving no room for confusion or chaos.

Though it is debated that men and women belong to different cultures in terms of their expectations out of communication, we will focus mainly on cross-cultural communication based on the following parameters.

- Ethnic background
- Socio-economic status
- Age
- Education level

Why is it important to understand cross-cultural communication?

Cross-cultural communication is crucial to be a successful employee. Because of the growth of global businesses and technologies today, this is of strategic importance not just for MNCs but all other companies as well.

Understanding this concept will keep confusion at bay because business requires us to meet, connect, negotiate and communicate with individuals from different cultures, countries and background. Since we all perceive the business world in different ways, it is a healthy practice to understand and appreciate these differences.

For instance, when we travel abroad for the first time, we realize the need to be more open and embrace other cultures. We need to understand that our own culture is not universally accepted, and the more open we are to other cultures and ideas, the more confident we can become. Being rigid is a big hurdle and one should avoid this, especially at the workplace.

Strategies to improve cross-cultural communication

1. *Speak slowly:* The number one tip is to speak slowly. The business world is already loaded with so many complexities

and problems, your pace of speech could add more to it and do a lot of damage. So when you are meeting and working with a diverse workforce, keep this simple yet useful tip in mind.

2. *Do not use slang:* Always remember to use professional and business-like language. Never resort to using slang — this could offend someone and it could cost you your business. Never take chances and assume that your counterpart will understand the latest slang in your personal dictionary!

3. *Politeness is the key:* When in doubt, always use words such as please, sorry and thank you. These are universally accepted. It is normal to be nervous or get confused when in an alien setting, workplace or country, with people from different cultural backgrounds. But one simple rule to remember is that we are all humans — politeness is appreciated by everyone. So when in doubt, always rely on your good manners.

4. *Listen:* Since we are talking about communication, we should not forget the importance of active listening. This means that you must be constantly involved and also acknowledge the speaker. In case of any confusion, ask a question or request the speaker to rephrase.

5. *KISS (Keep It Simple and Short):* Remember, communication helps us to connect better and build trust. To achieve this goal, always talk to the point.

6. *Put in a little effort:* Everything is easily available in this age of Google. So, if your work demands that you must meet and interact with people from cultures other than your own, put in some extra effort and learn about their cultures. For instance, if you are required to connect with a team of German experts in the aerospace field, it is a

good idea to study a little bit about their culture and their lifestyle. This small piece of information can take you a long way in connecting and building trust.

Many big organizations delegate the task of training to the HR team that provides in-depth cross-cultural training to better understand cultural differences between nations. This, I believe, is a great tool, because not only does it help employees better understand new tasks but also adds to their confidence level while interacting with their counterparts from other countries and cultures and avoid potential cultural faux pas.

However, if your company is not able to provide the basic training, you can always do this on your own. It will always prove beneficial.

We all evolve with time, and the same applies to cross-cultural communication and gender roles. We are all becoming more open and believe in the power of communication, which is a product of our culture and socialization. So be open—ask questions when in doubt.

11

How to Keep the Passion Going

You can do anything as long as you have the passion, the drive, the focus, and the support.
— Sabrina Bryan

I prefer to see my work as my passion because the term 'work' is often loaded with burden.

It is critical to clearly define these terms because we tend to perceive things as we define them. Some very ordinary and mundane aspects of our lives actually take up a majority of our time. For instance, what is life? What is work? What is passion?

The mental definitions we have of words such as work, life and passion directly impinge upon our perceptions of these terms and the quality of life we lead.

As a freelance trainer and a writer, I never feel I am at work—I always feel that I am growing my creative side and improving my craft with each passing day. When I don't improve my craft and stop learning new things, I feel that the meaning of my life is diminishing. Do you feel the same way when you are not working or if you are out of your workplace for long for some reason?

Answer these questions to understand if you are passionate about your work.

- Do you never think of taking long breaks from your workplace?

- Do you feel that push to do something better than you have done before?
- Does your work/craft make you feel happy, not just at the end of the day, but at all times?

The answers to these questions are very powerful. It will help you understand if you are really passionate about doing the things you do.

If you have answered 'Yes' to all three questions, you are a happy professional. You work for happiness and contentment, things that are beyond comfort, luxury and the money you earn.

But even if you have answered 'No' to any of the three questions above, it is not a problem. Remember all problems come with solutions. Let us learn how to turn these 'Nos' into a big 'Yes'.

Step 1: Define Love and Your Passion

When you define what you love and what your passion is, you will know what keeps you happy. The very essence of our lives is based upon 'happiness'. Everything we do, or struggle to achieve, ultimately has something to do with this intangible part of our lives—happiness. This idea is beautifully shown in one of my all-time favourite films *The Pursuit of Happiness*.

So, knowing what keeps you happy within is the first step towards keeping your passion alive.

Step 2: Define Work

Now define 'work', or what you do for a living.

If it is not same as your passion, ask yourself another question: Why I do what I do? If you cannot find a convincing reason, it is time to rethink what you do.

If you don't find happiness in your work, it will become

a burden. Finding a reason that keeps you happy is essential because work has to be either done for happiness or for some other strong purpose.

Step 3: Stop Looking for External Praise

The key is to crave for internal satisfaction—not success or achievement.

According to me, success is something that is external and is equivalent to the popularity we gain for our work. As a true professional, you should not yearn for success—rather, your aim should be to set your own targets and go about reaching them. This means you must celebrate baby steps too. Achievement should be about self-discovery—it should be internal, or how you perceive your craft, work or passion. When you achieve something, reward yourself and don't go looking for external approvals.

Step 4: Record the New Things You Learn

As humans we have a tendency to count our problems rather than our blessings. We need to work consciously to change this attitude, and an easy way to remind ourselves about all the good and beautiful things in our professional life is to record them on a piece of paper and then transfer them to our minds, hearts and souls. This will always keep us happy and strong.

For instance, make it a regular habit to record all good things about your professional life every Sunday morning. If you are very busy, then try to do this at least once a month. Personally, weekly notes work for me because they help me record every little blessing in my life and recharge me for the coming week.

This simple activity will help you steer away from the negative things and focus only on the positive.

Step 5: Coach and Help Others

I was once asked in an event organized by MBA students as to why I have taken up writing as my career.

I replied, 'I totally believe in my work and when I have something so good with me, I can't let it just sit with me. It shall dance, sing, fly and connect hearts!'

So, when you are passionate about what you do, until you share it and connect with others, you will not see its real beauty. Sharing ideas and helping others by sharing insights will give you immense joy—one that will not be found if you work alone. I find coaching and helping others is a great way to keep the passion alive—it is a simple act, but it has the potential to change a life for the better! Remember this positive ripple effect and try to help others, not for the sake of tangible benefits but because some things ought to be done just for the sake of goodness.

12

How to Negotiate

> *The most difficult thing in any negotiation, almost, is making sure that you strip it of the emotion and deal with the facts.*
>
> —Howard Baker

Before we begin to understand negotiation in detail, let us try and understand how much time we spend on negotiating in our lives.

10%
50%
Over 90%

The answer is: all the time!

Yes, it is true that we are negotiating all the time, often without even realizing it. We do it at work, at home, during our travels, and even on a holiday we are negotiating! In fact, the entire world is a big 'stage for negotiation', and we are all 'negotiators' busy negotiating all the time, no matter what our role is. As a parent, as a teacher, as a child, or as a professional, we are all trying hard to achieve our own interests.

It is worth knowing more about negotiation because negotiation skills play a very critical role in the business context. As a corporate trainer, I have always wondered why is it that we coach and educate professionals about a range of hard and soft skills, but do not stress upon the importance of negotiation skills that are mandatory for success in the workplace. Let us first define what is negotiation.

Negotiation is a formal process in which discussions between people or groups (with different aims) take place in order to try to reach an agreement or find a common ground, where both groups are satisfied and reach their desired aims (mutually acceptable agreement). In this process, each individual or group tries to gain more benefit than the other.

While you analyse the definition, do not confuse 'negotiation' with 'bargaining' — or what I call 'Big B'.

Let us understand the one major difference between bargaining and negotiating. While you might think your mother to be a great bargainer, she might not be a good negotiator. This is because bargaining is limited to the 'price' of the product and most of us are pretty good at bargaining, because it is limited to one thing only — money. Negotiation, on the other hand, involves many other factors like dignity, status, security, and so on. It may not include the 'money' element at all.

For example, when two big shots are trying to win a deal for better 'status' — not for 'money' — how would they compromise or negotiate? In this case, the negotiation is for 'interest' and not money.

I recall one of my professors showing a small audio-visual clip in management class about two goats and a bridge. It was an introduction to the chapter on negotiation. Each goat tried crossing a narrow bridge before the other but every time they fell into the river. Finally, they decided to work on their 'interests' after keeping their egos aside. This way they were able to come to an agreement of crossing the bridge one by one.

Hence, negotiation is not about arguing and fighting; it is all about coming to a win–win situation where both parties leave happily.

It is easier to negotiate when you understand the interest of the opponent individual or party, and also clearly understand the stages involved in negotiation. Broadly speaking, we can divide a negotiation process into three stages:

Three Stages of Negotiation

1. *Prepare and present*: Negotiation process begins by understanding not just what we want but also understanding what value this process holds for the opponent. Some key points to remember are:
   - Know what you want
   - Know what your opponent wants
   - Collect data and gain complete knowledge about your need
   - Show value and try to understand the opponent's interest
2. *Discussion*: In this stage, the real give and take happens, in which communication plays a crucial role and the haggling takes place. This is a good sign of any negotiation process.

   Let us assume a simple scenario of a seller and buyer: The seller attempts to get all sorts of clues from the buyer. A good seller will talk less at this stage and instead get the buyer to reveal his cards. He will ask probing questions, listen more and try to make the negotiation process free from all hurdles.
3. *Conclusion*: A positive negotiator is in fact closing the deal from the very beginning. From the very moment you present the first point of your proposal, you should believe that you will walk away with the deal. It is seen that having a positive attitude helps one sound assertive, clear and focused.

   Though this attitude is good, it is not always easy to

close a deal and get what you expect from the negotiation process. Hence, it is necessary to also understand the 'walk away point', as this is the minimum requirement and flexibility you should be open to. When you are asked to be more flexible, it is advised that you walk away from the deal rather than settle for something far lower than your expectation. So, knowing your walk away point will keep you in the game and even if you walk away, you will be not at the losing end.

Seven Golden Strategies to Win at Negotiations

1. *Know what you want*: Clarity is key in negotiation. The entire process of negotiation depends on the clarity of individuals (or concerned parties) on what they want out of the negotiation process. This means that you must know what outcome you want. Once you envision it, it helps you to steer your discussion towards that goal.
2. *Communicate assertively*: You will get what you want when you express yourself clearly. Being assertive is a quality that every negotiator should develop. When you talk assertively, it shows your knowledge and expertise, and this lets you stay in a stronger position while keeping the other party on their heels.
3. *Asking questions*: Though questions are an integral part of the entire negotiation process, questioning skills are indispensable during the discussion stage.
   These questions can help us understand the process better:
   - What does the opponent want?
   - How flexible are they? This could mean understanding their 'best alternative to a negotiated agreement' (BATNA).
   - How can you reach a win–win agreement?

Once you have a list of these questions, it is easier to understand the interest of the opponent and then it becomes easier to win the negotiation.

4. *Active listening*: While it is good to communicate assertively, and ask the right questions, we must not forget that in the negotiation process, active listening is key. So, during the entire negotiation process, remember to speak less and listen more actively. This means you must acknowledge your opponent, make a note of their body language and also read between the lines. This will help you glean clues, making the whole negotiation process easier.

   In most big-stake negotiations, many parties take along a few members, who are just actively listening and observing the opponents' body language. They help the team understand the opponent better and play a crucial role in closing the deal. So, one thing to learn here is that it is always better to have the support of a team, rather than going all alone and trying to do it all by yourself.

5. *Do your homework*: Information is power in negotiation; the more informed you are the more power you have in your hands to negotiate. Knowledge and practice will always keep you ahead of your opponent. Hence, it is highly recommended that before going to the negotiation table, a quick recap of possible questions and discussions can help you a great deal. As discussed previously, envisioning the outcome is positive affirmation, and a practical way to do this is through role play with your team in advance. This will prepare you thoroughly for the deal, and even if things do not shape up exactly as you planned, it will help you stay focused.

6. *Build rapport*: Sometimes we tend to get into the grip of 'demands and pressure', and we start thinking too

technically and forget that we are negotiating with humans. We begin to treat them like machines and a point comes where we are not able to close the deal even though we had a good chance to do this. This can happen, especially when we fail to connect and empathize with the opponent party members. Remember that we are all emotional beings and things can be simplified if we give respect and listen to them and also try to understand their point of reference. Always stay high on your emotional quotient (EQ) — only if you give a little can you expect to get something in return.

7. *Walk away point*: Even though a negotiation process usually begins on a positive note, it is not always possible to get what you want. So, be ready to 'walk away' when you realize that you cannot possibly reach an agreement with the other side. The most important thing here is to walk away with dignity, even if you are not able to close the deal. But only when you clearly know what you want is it possible to walk away with clarity and no ill feelings.

I believe that these rules will help you appear more confident and talk assertively during negotiations. I recommend you to read and watch a few videos by Alan McCarthy who helped numerous Fortune 100 companies such as Oracle and Microsoft to smartly handle negotiations.

Some Important Terms in Negotiation

- *Counter offer:* Rejecting the previous offer and offering a new one with new terms
- *BATNA:* Best Alternative to a Negotiated Agreement
- *Anchoring bias:* Relying too much on the first offer and then using this piece of information like a reference point or an anchor upon which the entire negotiation process revolves

- *Status quo:* An emotional bias that affects the decision-making process. This mainly applies to the family negotiation process. In this scenario, one may let go of a negotiation because he/she gives greater importance to the relationship (or closeness) with the other than one's personal interest

13

How to Set Goals

You have to dream, before your dreams come true.
— A.P.J. Abdul Kalam

Setting Goals

Think about great speakers on the TEDx platform—one of the greatest platforms to share ideas and inspirations for people around the world. Think about a student who wants to qualify a competitive exam or an athlete who is trying to win a gold medal for his/her nation. What is the common thing between the two? A clear goal.

Be it a TEDx speaker, a student or an athlete, the common thing that ties them together is that they have a dream, a target and a goal. Similarly, once you set a goal, it gives you the drive to accomplish what you have dreamt of. After you decide your goal, the next step is to visualize it. Visualization is a very strong tool—it is to see images of what you really want to accomplish in your life. Once you picture yourself achieving your dream, there is no force that can hold you back. Let us go over the steps you need to follow to chase your goals.

Step 1: It sounds so easy to say 'Think' about a goal (and just go all out and achieve it!). But, I am not suggesting that you should randomly pick a goal.

I recommend this filter (I call it ABV) to help set your

goals. This filter has three criteria that will help you check the relevance of your goal.

A = Altruistic
B = Beneficial
V = Value

Let us understand this acronym in terms of importance.

'V' stands for value, and with this layer you will check if your goal is in sync with your values, principles and passion as you will give your best only when you feel passionate about your goal. If you are setting up a goal that your value system does not support or you don't believe in wholeheartedly, it is better you abort the goal at the very outset.

'B' stands for beneficial. This means that while setting up a goal, you must check whether your goal has the power to benefit you professionally or personally in a meaningful way. It could be a goal to enhance your skills, or one to better you as an individual or even help you emotionally or mentally.

'A' stands for altruistic, and this mean that while setting up a goal, you should remember not to be selfish or egocentric. Always set a goal that will not just benefit you but also others (or at least one that does no harm to others).

If your goal survives these three layers, then you can proceed to Step 2.

Step 2: Think in images.
Before I jump to explaining this step to you, I would like you to close your eyes for 10 seconds and imagine your goal.

Did you imagine it?

How do you feel now?

I am sure a few adjectives like 'positive', 'encouraging', 'realistic' and so on, come to mind.

Images have this extreme power to connect us to our

future goals. They inspire us and encourage us to stay focused.

Step 3: Write down in detail about your goals. You will be so amazed at the positive power of setting goals. Doing this will double your motivation, and when you write down your goals, it will give you clarity as to what steps must be followed to achieve your goals. Remember, when you 'ink it, you think it'.

Things to remember when you write down your goals:

1. Make them realistic
2. Keep them simple. If they are very complicated, break them into simple short-term goals. For example, your goal should not be: 'I want to be a true professional', because that is a very vague goal. Instead, it would be wise to break them into simpler steps, such as:
   » First, I shall work on my dressing sense
   » Then, I will work on my etiquette
   » Finally, I will work on my communication skills

So, in this step, you must write down your goals clearly and uncomplicate them (if needed).

So, go all out, with full determination, and write down your goals.

Step 4: Remember to measure and review because you can only improve those things that can be measured. So, if you are not able to measure a goal, you cannot improve it.

In this step, you should focus on measuring your goals. You must also ensure that you are able to review them timely.

Let us talk about 'Measure'. It is only when you measure your goals that you are able to track them, and this makes it easier to know if you have deviated from them. One way to do this is to measure your goals in terms of time taken. For example, you may want to improve your dressing sense to look more professional within 15 days. To achieve this, your strategy can be to invest in appropriate formal clothes for yourself.

By doing this, you have two measurable parameters to help you achieve your goal:

» 15 days' time
» Amount invested in purchasing branded formal clothing

In addition to measuring and tracking, you must also review your goal from time to time (in this case, within 15 days).

To do this, you can stick to two review dates—one after 5 days and another after 10 days, and while reviewing your goal if you feel that you are still very far from improving your dressing sense then you can consider taking the help of a professional.

So, whether goals are short term or long term, it is essential that you must review them in a timely manner and also set a ceiling as to when you will accomplish them.

A simple format is suggested here. You can modify it to suit your own needs and requirements. But however you do it, remember that the most crucial element is how much you are investing in your goals. Be honest and committed to them.

Start date	My goal: To get a job in a good organization
Review date 1	[fill in date when you first review your goal]
Review date 2	
Review date 3	
Completion date	Reward I will get: [Surprise yourself with some reward after achieving your goal/s]

Now, it's your turn to write down below about your goal and keep reviewing it every week.

Start date:	My goal:
Review date 1:	
Review date 2:	
Review date 3:	
Completion date:	Reward I will get:

In other words it means you are able to quantify your goals and track them. When you measure your goals it will help you to understand how far or close you are from your desired goal.

If you feel you are very far from your desired goal, you should change your goal steps or ways to achieve and rework on your strategy to accomplish the goal, and on the other hand, if you see that you are very close to reaching your goal, you are positively stimulated and hence you achieve your goal before time.

If your goal is to improve your dressing sense, you may keep your deadline of 15 days with two review dates to measure if you are on track and will be able to really achieve your goal of improving your dressing sense in the next 15 days.

So you may keep your first review date to measure it after 5 days (from the start date of your goal) and then again a second review after 5 days to measure and track your goal.

And while doing the first or second review if you notice that you are not reaching towards your goal, then perhaps you will change your strategy and think of taking a professional's help to achieve your goal in time.

Step 5: This is the art of execution. After having set clear goals, writing them down, and measuring and reviewing them, it is also necessary to execute them. Execution is a very difficult and hard path to tread.

Sometimes it may happen that after you measure your goals and review them, you feel as though your goal is impossible to achieve. This may dishearten you and you may decide to give up. But remember, when things seem impossible or very difficult, it is actually just a sign that you need to rethink your way to achieve your goal. You must rework on your strategies but not change the goal.

Always keep three things in mind when you feel like quitting:

1. Remember to focus
2. Ignite your passion
3. Rethink your approach

It is good to question when you are stuck, but you need to remember to question the approach and not your ability or the goal.

In fact, asking relevant questions can help you reach your goal. Let us see what could be a few relevant questions to ask in this scenario.

'Relevant questions give you relevant answers.'

This is a very powerful line. To stay focused on your goals and achieve them, answer these questions in the space provided below.

How important are my goals to me?
_____
_____
_____

What will help me achieve my goals? (knowledge/skill/attitude)
_____
_____
_____

Who (manager coach, superiors or someone else) can help me achieve my goals?
_____
_____
_____

What will I need in order to gain support or convince them?
_____
_____
_____

Who else do I need to involve? (team/organization/institution/society)
_____
_____
_____

What do I need in terms of resources?
_____
_____
_____

Where is the action required and what will be my milestones?
_____
_____
_____

How will I measure my progress?
_____
_____
_____

Who will I involve in reviewing my progress?
_____
_____
_____

What and who can prevent me from achieving my goals?
_____
_____
_____

What action steps will I take to prevent the breakdown?
_____
_____
_____

14

How to Create Workplace Dos and Don'ts

Civility costs nothing and buys everything.
—Mary Wortley Montagu

An individual must know how to behave at the workplace. There is a huge difference between college and professional life. You need to be highly disciplined at work. Remember you can't behave the same way at your workplace as you do at home. You need to be professional and organized.

It is important to be well-behaved to earn respect and appreciation. Although basic business etiquette may remain the same all over the world, a few principles may vary from country to country and between cultures. Remember that the culture of a company is its soul, and therefore forms the basis of the Dos and Don'ts of the organization. Having said that, there are few rules that are considered global and are accepted (and followed) all over the world.

The main reason for having a list of Dos and Don'ts is to clearly state what is right and what is not as per company policy. While these may come naturally to some people, others may have to be told well in advance. Sharing this list is the responsibility of the HR department.

21 Dos and Don'ts at Work

1. Having a casual attitude towards work is a complete no-no. Realize that you cannot ever afford to bring in your casual attitude to the workplace because you are being paid to work and not for loitering around.
2. Always mind your own business. Before you become a good team player, you must first concentrate and complete your job on time. So don't waste time walking up to your colleagues for casual chats or gossip sessions. Also, remember to respect privacy.
3. There should be no loud noises from your digital companions. Loud ringtones are very unprofessional and also disturb others around you. So no matter how smart your device is, keep the volume low.
4. Never criticize or make fun of your colleagues. If there is a problem, the key to solving it is through communication. Sit down and talk face-to-face. Always remember that petty people gossip about other people; important people talk about inspiration and aspiration.
5. Stay away from mean politics at the workplace. Avoid playing blame games and gossiping.
6. Keep your workstation clean and tidy.
7. Never shout at anyone and take care of your pitch and tone at the workplace. It is unprofessional to lash out at others, and if someone does it, report it immediately to the senior management.
8. Make it a habit to attend meetings or seminars with a notepad and pen. It is a small thing but very helpful.
9. Be punctual, and reach office on time. Discipline must be maintained at the workplace.
10. Gentlemen, remember to *not* dress in casuals. No organization likes shabbily dressed employees. Shave daily

and do not use strong perfumes.
11. Ladies, make sure you never wear revealing clothes to work. Stick to minimal make-up and avoid wearing heavy jewellery.
12. Never pass lewd comments on your fellow workers.
13. While having lunch together, eat slowly to avoid burping in public.
14. Respect your fellow workers and help them whenever required.
15. Know what is yours and what is not — office stationery is meant to be used only at work and if you are in the habit of taking them home, it is equivalent to stealing.
16. Always carry your business card with you and keep them in a business card case.
17. Be cost effective and eco-friendly — do not waste water and electricity. Remember to switch off your system before you leave for the day; turn off the fans, air-conditioning, lights and other electronic devices such as printer, fax machine, scanner, and so on. Also ensure that you do not leave taps open in the washroom.
18. Pay attention where to park your vehicle so that it does not create trouble for others.
19. Smoke only at the designated smoking zones.
20. While it is okay to sneeze or cough in public, always use a handkerchief or tissue to cover your mouth.
21. No chewing gums — it is okay to do this while in college, but is not expected of a professional.

This list will not only help you stay like a true professional but also help you look more classy and refined.

15

How to Do SWOT Analysis

> *Spending too much time focused on others' strengths leaves us feeling weak. Focusing on our own strengths is what, in fact, makes us strong.*
> —Simon Sinek

What Is SWOT Analysis?

SWOT analysis is a planning technique used to help a person or an organization identify their Strengths, Weaknesses, Opportunities and Threats (SWOT) viz-a-viz business competition.

I am a strong admirer of this simple yet effective tool of personality development. Having worked on your communication and business etiquette skills, it is now time to introspect and also do your own SWOT analysis. The main purpose of this is to amplify strength, overcome weaknesses, exploit opportunities and minimize threats.

Let us now do a SWOT analysis to learn more about ourselves. In the box below, fill in at least five points under each of the four columns.

My Balance Sheet: SWOT Analysis	
My Assets	My Liabilities
My Strengths Example: I hold an MBA degree 1. 2. 3. 4. 5.	**My Weaknesses** Example: No practical exposure 1. 2. 3. 4. 5.
My Opportunities Example: To gain experience in the world of work 1. 2. 3. 4. 5.	**My Threats** Example: Fitting into company culture 1. 2. 3. 4. 5.

This exercise will give you clarity about what to do next. The example provided for strength is having an MBA degree. Remember that each strength will give you an opportunity; so, recognize that opportunity and explore more options to grow. For example, if you have an MBA degree, you have won an opportunity to work and gain experience that other students might not have.

Moving on to the next column: 'what is your weakness?' The example shows 'no practical exposure'. Just the way each strength gives you an opportunity, in the same way, every weakness will be like a threat. If you already recognize that threat, you have sorted 50 per cent of your problems because you can now be prepared with a contingency plan. So, again, if you look at the example, the weakness is not having any practical exposure in the corporate world. Hence, the biggest threat is: 'will you be able to adjust to corporate culture?' Once you realize the problem you might encounter, you can be ready to combat and overcome the threat.

Make your own list and watch out for great opportunities coming your way, and at the same time, also be ready to combat the threats you might encounter.

Remember that if you keep working on your strengths and master them, no weakness will stand in the way of your success.

When to Perform SWOT Analysis

One can do the SWOT analysis as and when the need arises; however, many of my students do a SWOT analysis on a quarterly basis or every six months. Whenever you feel the need to revisit and work on your SWOT—or if you have to make a significant decision—feel free to do sit down and work on your SWOT. This analysis works like a self-audit system that tells you if you are going off track and lets you know where you stand in the market in terms of your strengths.

16

How to Lead

> *A man who wants to lead the orchestra must turn his back on the crowd.*
>
> —Max Lucado

Ethics and Passion

Though most of the time we use the words 'ethics' and 'morals' interchangeably, it is very important to know the difference between the two. Ethics are external—they evolve with society and can be understood as rules that one must adhere to. For instance, they could be workplace rules to be followed by professionals or religious principles. Morals, on the other hand, are internally driven. They recommend what is wrong or right according to our individual principles.

Having understood this subtle difference, let us now discuss who is an ethically passionate leader (EPL).

Ethically Passionate Leader

I like to define leadership as a combination of these two rare qualities (ethics and passion), and I admire leaders whom I call EPLs. I have seen a few great leaders excel and grow because they have very high standards of morals and ethics, and at the same time are passionate about the work they do.

It is easy to find passionate leaders; however, when you are clouded by passion you tend to be ethically blind. There are a rare few leaders who have the capacity and potential not to be blinded by their passion and they are the true leaders—the EPLs. Not only do they care for people and the world around while creating waves through their passion, they are also ethically sound.

Our world today needs more EPLs—those who let others grow along with them. An EPL inspires not just through his work but also through his vision, which is clear, just and ethically sound. This type of leader begins by creating a vision for all that is communicated to everyone in the system. The vision is embedded with strong corporate cultural values as well as dignity and equality.

An EPL clearly describes three stages for any big or small decision to be taken at the workplace.

The decision is considered, only if it is ethically viable at the first stage. At the second stage, it is filtered on the scale of passion, and if it passes this filter, the decision is then made a part of the system.

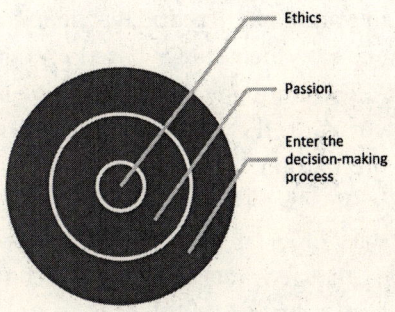

Graph by Anu Manhotra

Two examples
Today, there are numerous educational institutes and many edupreneurs—these edupreneurs are successfully running so-called educational institutes. Now the question arises whether

or not they are successful in terms of improving the quality of education imparted to students or are they merely successful in terms of making profits?

The most important thing to understand here is what these edupreneurs are passionate about. Is it education or business? Because schools, colleges and institutes are openly minting money, it can be said that they are only passionate about profit-making and are ethically blind. They do not care how their passion for money is killing the present and future of our younger generations. In fact, their ethical blindness endangers the soul of the entire system. It is not far-fetched to say that all educational institutes should confirm to very high standard of ethics. But this can only happen when there are great leaders at the top.

Let us look at another scenario—a mobile app design company. Imagine that this company is passionate about incorporating the latest technology in their apps, and they wish to carve a niche for themselves in the teen market sector. This company has an option of attracting teenagers with an app that will help them choose their career based on their responses to a questionnaire. The company, however, knows that no matter what the answers are, the questionnaire will be biased and recommend only certain institutes or colleges that will pay them a big price in exchange of sensitive data. If the mobile app company has EPLs, it will disregard this lucrative offer (despite the fact that it wants to carve a niche in this sector), because it finds it to be ethically blind.

This simple model gives power to ethical practices at the workplace, thereby making the world a better place. We need to remember that even if we are very passionate about something, we need to first screen our ideas on the basis of ethics.

What You Should Do

In an ethically blind society, morals are those strong roots that will help you grow anywhere and everywhere. Those who lack morals are only able to work with like-minded people, and once they are cut off from that corrupt system, they lack roots to grow back to life again.

- Creating a brand does not mean that you go with the flow or blindly follow trends. It means: be you, be authentic.
- People will always remember you for your brand; so create a beautiful you, without aping others. Try to be a great EPL.
- Do not chase name and fame; just work, grow and let others also grow with you. Remember EPLs are those who never crave to be at the front but they help others. It is okay to be unnoticed sometimes, and this can happen in the corporate world too.
- When you work from your heart with strong morals and a clean character, you don't just create a brand, you create a legacy.

Case Study on Ethical Blindness

This case study is not related to a business concept or a system, but is in fact closely embedded in us—our individual values, principles and strengths.

Read the case study and try to understand the issue of 'ethical blindness' in the business world.

> *BREAKING NEWS:*
> *Yet another big corporate turns out to be a scandalous one!*
> *Yet another corporate giant leader is convicted on the grounds of being ethically corrupt!*

Why is it that we are hearing so many stories of the corporate world growing ethically blind?

Is it the modern fear of not being at the peak always, or to find a way into the Forbes list, that makes these corporate giants fall into dark, dirty pits filled with the soot of selfish greed and endless needs?

Is it right to blame modern complexities and tough competition for rising levels of ethical blindness?

Do you agree or disagree?

I will not give an answer; instead I will call upon the 'ghost' of ethical blindness from the past, and present to you some examples that will allow you to decide for yourself.

How many of you remember the Ford Pinto story?

In 1970, the small car market in the US was facing severe competition from German cars such as the Volkswagen Beetle. So, the American car manufacturing company Ford decided to give tough competition to the Germans by bringing to the market a very affordable 'small car'. This car was manufactured in record time, and in just 25 months the Pinto was ready to be sold. Though it was a good-looking car, there was something about it that was damaging, and even life-threatening.

Ford knew about its faulty gas tank design but decided to ignore it, just to get ahead of the Germans without worrying about the lives of the people who bought the car. Ford was completely ethically blind in his decision to market the Pinto.

Some statistics estimate that Pinto crashes caused up to 500 burn deaths that could have been avoided, had it not been for the faulty gas tanks bursting into flames. Others estimate this number at 900! 'Burning Pintos' shook many in the US in the 1970s. Ultimately, Ford had to pay millions of dollars in lawsuits to victims and their families.

Many such sad examples exist even in the noblest of professions such as medicine. For example, cases of fake medical degrees, organ theft by doctors and other horrifying stories exist.

In the Indian context, the Satyam Computer Services scandal comes to mind. This was a corporate scandal that occurred in India in 2009 in which Chairman Ramalinga Raju confessed that the company's accounts had been falsified. This is interesting to me because no one in the Board of Directors—all highly experienced professionals—had come forth to stop the owner from going down the wrong path. This brings me to another concept that must be understood: Abilene Paradox.

An Abilene Paradox is one in which a group of people collectively decide on a course of action, even when not all in the group agree with the decision. In other words, if you know something is wrong but don't stand up and say so, just because nobody else is speaking up, it is an Abilene Paradox. Simply put, it is a desire to *not* 'rock the boat'.

In the case of the Satyam Scam too, there was no whistleblower, even though they may have known that the company was taking an unethical path.

Therefore, the lesson learnt from the past (and in the current context) is that when you know you are right, find the courage to stand up and take, what I call, the 'moral chair'. Do not be afraid of being alone when you say the truth.

Make a promise to yourself today that you will not allow ethical blindness in the corporate world, neither as an individual nor as group. As management students and management trainers, we must know the basics of Manage/me/nt as 'Manage Me' and then 'Manage/men/t', i.e., Manage Men.

List out the main points discussed in this chapter.

Share or describe if you have faced the 'Abilene Paradox' in your work life or elsewhere.

17

How to Learn and Stay Ahead

Develop a passion for learning. If you do, you will never cease to grow.
— Anthony J. D'Angelo

Be pro-active', 'it is a competitive world', 'take up more responsibilities', 'raise the banner' are some of the phrases we often hear. Most relate these to one thing and that is staying ahead, while others equate it with promotions.

It is always good to grow, but if you only seek growth in terms of positions and titles, they will soon stop attracting you, as real growth is beyond titles. When we grow to learn more and serve more, we reach greater professional heights.

Let us check out some great ways to grow along this path.

World of Blogs

As a writer and corporate trainer, I recommend blogs as a great way to gain deep knowledge on a subject of interest. Bloggers write out of passion and it is this passion that makes them give their best. So you can always enhance your knowledge by reading blogs that are rich in content. You can follow such blogs and stay up to date.

Also when you gain expertise, you can start your own blog wherein you can ink your own thoughts. Blogging can unleash many creative ideas. If you become a regular blogger, you also tend to stay updated because it becomes your responsibility to share the latest piece of information with your readers. Blogging is a great way to stay ahead.

Knowledge-sharing Sessions

Knowledge is power only when shared. The more knowledge you share, the more you grow. This holds true even in the corporate arena. Many believe that sharing is powerful mainly in terms of business knowledge, and wait for someone else to take the initiative. This is not ideal and will not allow you to achieve what you desire.

So the golden rule to stay ahead is to share your knowledge, and not be a hoarder. Take initiative without waiting (or hoping) that someone from the leadership or top executive level will raise the banner for you. Instead, take charge. Once you do this, you are already leading and marching ahead of others. By sharing knowledge and creating platforms for the same, you will inspire others in the organization and you will no longer be an ordinary employee.

Tips on Knowledge Sharing

- *Knowledge management*: As a true professional, you must understand what is knowledge management policy. Also all the employees must be aware of the fact that knowledge hoarding is unprofessional. In other words, if an employee possesses or learns a skill that is useful at work and for other team members, but he/she is not willing to share, it is knowledge hoarding and no true professional should ever do this.
- *Organize fun social activities*: The more you socialize as a team, the more you communicate with each other. This leads to creativity as you are connected with each

other. An easy way to do this is through regular team socializing activities or events.

For instance, when one engineering employee travels to Germany for a year to understand more about aerospace manufacturing, he/she can conduct a short session for the team on returning. Other employees can learn about the Dos and Don'ts at the Germany manufacturing plant, so that when the next batch or group of engineers travels for business, they can take their insights from this knowledge-sharing session (KSS).

- *Latest technology*: KSS is all about more interaction and collaboration; however, you must understand that you can make use of the latest technology too, as this will act as a platform to get you started. As a true professional, you must know the latest software for KSS, so that every employee is able to access information for getting the work done. Some examples of such softwares are Guru, Bitrix 24 and Inkling Knowledge. The best thing about KSS is that it actually strengthens internal communication and helps to connect within the organization, thereby making it a more productive and happier workplace.

The Power of Massive Open Online Learning Courses

Massive Open Online Learning (MOOC) is a platform for learning, sharing and growing. What I like most about MOOC is that it is not only an online platform where knowledge is assimilated. Instead, it is a shared learning process, where innumerable courses and subjects are available wherefrom keen learners such as you or I can choose a course of our choice. If you are working as a CAD/CAM engineer and you feel you need to work on a specific area to gain expertise, then you can simply enrol in that particular course.

You can also choose a short-term or long-term course, based on your interest and availability. The best part about the global MOOC is that it allows you to connect with students from the world over. For example, if you want to learn more about improving your speaking skills, you can enrol in that specific course—not just that, you also get to make new friends and meet other professionals with whom you can speak and exchange ideas, tips and strategies. All this will ultimately work towards building your collaborative learning skills as well. Best of all, this platform has both free and paid certification courses.

The two best-known websites for MOOC are www.coursera.com and www.edx.org

So choose MOOC, not just for certification but also to improve your life!

Attend a Professional Conference

Having talked in detail about online courses, I don't want to take away the importance of face-to-face interaction with peers and superiors from the business community. Attending events such as conferences will give you a great opportunity not just to learn but also to meet people—experts and novices within your business community. The entire experience can be very rewarding. I personally love to attend such conferences—it is not just about work, but also the connect with new, interesting people. Also, these conferences are great ways to stay updated with the latest happenings in your industry.

Job Rotation

What do we need as an employee other than monetary benefits and facilities? I would say, many things such as practical exposure, gaining expertise, climbing up the corporate ladder, being able to lead and guide others, and so on.

As you all know, retaining employees is a key issue for organizations. So how can companies cut down on their attrition and how can an employee always stay ahead?

The answer to this question is through broadening skill-sets. The best way to do this is through job rotation in the organization. This will help an employee gain experience in varied fields, grow as an overall professional, develop leadership qualities and fight boredom and monotony of a routine job. In short, job rotation enhances skills and leads to career development.

The best part of job rotation is that it keeps both management and the employee happy, so convincing your HR department for job rotation in their organization will be worth every penny.

As a professional, you need to always find ways to stay up to date and current, and also openly advice and suggest new inclusions in the current system. Remember that though one person cannot bring about complete change, a single person can usher in the revolution, so never hesitate to share your ideas.

18

How to Answer Top HR Questions

> *I had six honest serving men – they taught me all I knew:*
> *Their names were Where and What and When and Why*
> *and How and Who.*
>
> —Rudyard Kipling

How many of us really understand the term HR? HR stands for Human Resources. It is that branch of the organization that is responsible for hiring, training, retraining and administering employee-benefit programmes. It is the department charged with finding, screening and recruiting job applicants. Job seekers must approach the HR department to apply for a job in the organization.

Some of you, who are fresh graduates or young professionals, mush have faced an HR interview. It is very simple for those who are confident and clear about their goals. But for others, it can be a daunting experience because of lack of practice.

Having worked as an HR Head, let me tell you that there are no right or wrong answers in the HR interview round. How you present yourself and your attitude is what an HR personnel will be looking out for. This chapter provides some sample responses to common questions asked by the HR of a company. Of course these are not to be reproduced verbatim, but will provide you with a framework. You must edit and alter them based on your personality and life experience.

But before we get to the questions, let us understand the standard job selection process, especially for Indian MNCs or good companies that have an HR system in place. This flowchart provides the steps that an applicant must go through in order to be selected.

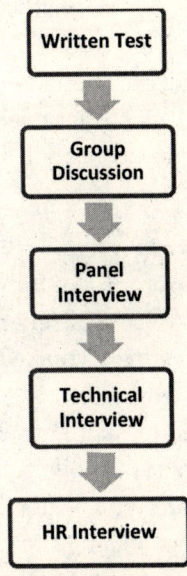

Sample Question and Answers

This is probably the final round (in most of the organizations), and your selection will depend on how well you answer these questions and how you carry yourself.

Question: 'How are you doing today?'
I am sure you expected something else, but I remember that I always used to ask the candidates this question first in order to break the ice.

Many would simply respond with a 'Fine' or 'Okay' or look confused.

This type of response shows that the candidate doesn't believe in interacting, and also reveals their lack of etiquette.

Remember this is actually not a question but just something to set the tone for the interview questions. Also this question helps candidates come out of their shell and become more comfortable.

When answering this question, use good or positive words. Every word that you speak carries energy—some positive, and others not so positive. So do not kill the positive energy; use some good adjectives.

Sample answer: I am doing great/brilliant/good. [Make sure you are use words appropriate for a professional setting. The words should carry a lot of energy and show that you are all out to interact, express yourself, learn more about the organization and your work role.]

What about manners?

If someone is asking you how you are doing, make sure you respond with a thank you. After all, the person opposite you has made an effort to enquire about you, so a small acknowledgement is due. So a perfect or near-perfect answer should sound like:

'I am doing great; thank you so much for asking.' [followed by a smile]

Practice the answer in front of a mirror. Say it out loud and clear. And, did you practice that with a smile?

Question: 'Tell me something about yourself.'

Despite this being one of the most commonly asked questions, many of us still dread and fumble when asked to talk about themselves.

Remember this question says 'something' — not everything about yourself. Understand that the main reason for asking this question is to check your presentation skills. They are also trying to find out if you will be an asset to the organization.

Begin with your academic or professional achievement that you are proud of, and then follow it up with your USP — your strengths.

Small things make a huge difference, so remember to use acknowledgements, such as 'Well', 'Okay', 'Sure', 'Ah ha', and so on. If you miss out on using acknowledging words, the HR interview will seem like a teacher questioning a small child!

Just imagine someone asking a child: What is your name? Gagan; Could you recite a rhyme? Johnny, Johnny, Yes Papa…

So you see, a child simply jumps into answering the question, without making a connection with the person asking questions. To avoid doing this, always use acknowledging words.

Remember, many can communicate; only few can connect.

So a perfect answer to this question would be something like this:

Sample answer: 'Well, I am Anu Manhotra and I have been in training for over 17 years. I have worked with various giants in the professional and corporate arena. My recent achievement is my writing craft and my main strength is my leadership ability and assertive communication skill.

You may also add what exactly you are looking for as an employee in the organization. You can say, 'What I am looking for is a company that values team work and recognizes and uses my strengths.'

If you are a fresher, you can say something on the lines of:

'Well, I am Aarti Singh. [If you have given your name earlier, do not start again with your name.] I did my B.Tech. in Electronics and Communications from Kaushal's College of Engineering, which is under PTU. I have represented my college in talent hunt and I strongly believe my strength lies in my communication and can-do attitude.

What I am looking for is a company that values team work and recognizes and uses my strengths. I have also done a thorough research about your company and I am glad to know that your company values leadership and I would indeed be proud to work for a company like yours.'

[Do not forget to do the research about the company, where you want to join and if possible also get to know about your job profile.]

[Do not talk about your family or hobbies until asked. Also, when talking about your strengths, keep it short and to the point.]

Question: 'Well, you have mentioned your strengths, now do tell us about your weakness.'

Again, remember to stay on the point; do not drag or talk too much and do not be extremely honest.

Sample answer: 'I am sure everyone has some good points and some not-so-good points. I too have a few areas that require improvement; however, I am sure my personal weaknesses will never affect my work. As a professional I have no weakness, but as a person I do.'

Close with a confident smile to show that in the professional arena you are willing to learn and be your best, even though at home (or in your personal life) you are just like anyone else.

Question: What are your hobbies?
Do not share all your hobbies, and especially avoid those that will not add charm to your professional image. Remember you are not talking to a family member or a friend, so do not pour your heart out. At the same time, do share a few relevant

hobbies that show your creative side.

Sample answer: 'Well, if I have to talk about my hobbies, I would say I love reading business journals and blogs related to my work. They help me stay up to date and add value to my work. Other than reading, I love exploring new places, travelling and meeting new people.'

If you have tons of hobbies, focus on two or three and not more.

Question: What motivates you?

Sample answer: 'Well, many things motivate me, but most of all, my goals and my mistakes motivate me. Goals help me to give my best and keep trying and mistakes are learning opportunities for me—they make me a stronger person. To me, a mistake is like a good teacher who encourages me to improve and better myself.'

Question: Don't you want to pursue higher studies? OR, Don't you think graduation is not sufficient? Do you not want to do your Masters?

By asking this question, the HR personnel wants to gauge your future plans, so answer this one smartly.

Sample answer: 'I strongly believe that more than any degree or certification, it is experience that teaches the most. Hence, I want to work in the real world and gain practical knowledge. Of course, learning from a structured course is also good and if needed in the near future and if I get a chance to enrol in an executive programme that conducts weekend classes, I will go for it. But as I said, I believe practical knowledge is key to success and confidence.'

[If you have done any internship, you can mention it here.]

Question: 'How do your friends/co-workers describe you?'

The intention behind this question is to understand how you score in terms of being a good team player. So relationships and your communication skills are something that you need to highlight in your response.

Sample answer: 'Up to date, eager beaver, smart-worker! I am a confident person, and these are a few adjectives that they will surely mention. I am a firm believer that one can never lead or grow alone, so I invest in professional relationships and I am a great team member who believes in sharing and learning, and of course, leading too.'

[Be confident when you use adjectives, but do not act oversmart.]

Question: 'How do you improve your knowledge base? You said that you like to keep yourself up to date; can you share with me what you have done in the last six months in this respect?'

Sample answer: 'Sure, this is a very good question as it gives me a chance to share with you my strategies to improve my knowledge. As I mentioned, I am an eager beaver and to stay current, I follow the latest and quick connecting tools so I enrolled myself in MOOC, which is a certification course offered online by coursers. It not only helped me to know more about my core subjects, but it also gave me a chance to meet students across the world and see where I stand on the world stage. Other than this, I always read the latest journals and magazines related to my subject.

[In order to stay up to date, it is advisable to join the latest online programmes. You can check out the MOOC courses.]

Question: What is your ideal company or workplace?

Sample answer: 'I believe any organization or workplace is organic in nature; it is not just a grand structure or a huge piece of architecture. For me the best place to work will be a place where I am always encouraged to grow, learn and share my ideas in an open environment where communication is not the power of a few, but all. Also, not to forget, my ideal place will be filled with new challenges, opportunities and greater goals.

Question: 'Could you share with us what has been the most difficult thing that you've accomplished so far? Or, what is the most difficult thing you have ever done?'

[Mention here how you have overcome your fear; it could be setting up a new business or helping your family to set up a business. It could even be something as simple as performing for the first time in a college event.]

Remember the question here is beginning with 'could', so always answer with acknowledging words such as 'of course', 'sure', 'absolutely' and so on.

Sample answer: 'Of course, I was never confident while speaking to foreigners, and last month in our college fest I got a chance to interact with a group of students from Germany. I also spoke to their lecturer and gave them a tour of the college. It was appreciated not just by them but also by all our college professors. So that was an accomplishment for me because it helped me come out of my shell.'

Question: 'Could you explain the difference between hard work and smart work?'

Sample answer: 'Sure, in simple words, hard work is all about effort while smart work is about putting lesser effort and more wit. As young educated students, we should not only depend upon hard work, but also use our wits and common sense to prioritize things and gets tasks done quickly and correctly.'

Question: 'Where do you see yourself in five years?'

Sample answer: 'Five years is a very long time and I am sure that I'll be in a strategic position in a reputed organization leading, learning, encouraging and training many youngsters.

Question: 'On a scale of 1 to 10, how would you rate yourself as a leader?'

Sample answer: '8.5, as there is so much more to learn, though I am a confident leader with a clear vision.'

[Always remember, KISS = Keep it Simple and Short. Only if you are asked to explain further should you share more about your leadership qualities. Perhaps talk about the time back in school or college when you led a team.]

Question: 'What are you most proud of?'

Sample answer: 'I don't think so far I've done something very laudable or praiseworthy—that moment is still pending for me.'

OR

'Once I land my first job. That will be a proud moment for sure.'

[If you have done something that you believe is great and commendable, share that confidently.]

Question: 'What has been your greatest failure?'

Sample answer: 'I believe that there is no such thing as "failure"; it is our mindset. And as I said previously, mistakes are great teachers. I have learnt in this journey called life that every experience, positive or negative, teaches us something and makes us better.'

Question: 'How do you manage time?'
[You can share some time management tips.]

Sample answer: 'I am highly organized and disciplined and follow simple yet impactful rules. No. 1 on my list is to make a to-do list. On the basis of the list, I then prioritize tasks as A, B, C.'

Question: 'How do you plan to work under pressure?'
OR
'Can you work under work pressure?'

Sample answer: 'Well, I believe if you work dutifully, there should be no pressure at all. However, if I have to work under pressure, it will certainly yield a positive outcome as working under pressure will be challenging; it will bring out the best in me.'

Question: 'Are you willing to relocate or travel?'
[Think before you talk—you know what your family wants from you.]
If they are comfortable with it, you can say:

Sample answer: 'Relocation should not be a problem for me. I would positively consider it, if the opportunity given to me is rewarding.'

Question: 'What do you know about us or our company?'
As mentioned previously, always do your homework about the company where you are being interviewed. Also, remember to read up about your job profile.

Sample answer: 'Well, after spending some time on your company's website, I now know that it is one of the finest and fastest-growing companies in India. Also, after going through the vision and mission statements, I feel positive about the work environment of your company. I know that it has been headed by great leaders since its very inception.'

[Add a few more facts about the company.]

Question: 'If we hire you, how long will you work for us?'

Sample answer: 'As a fresher, I am looking out to start with an organization that will help me transform into a true professional. I have set my mind to work and I have no thoughts of quitting the organization as long as there is growth in what I do. Also, I would like to stress here that I believe in long-term relationships, which will allow me to grow along with the organization.'

Question: 'How much salary do you expect?'

Sample answer: 'Well, the salary for my first job will be the learning experience. As a fresher, my priority is to improve my skills and I am sure the company has a set package for this post, so I am completely okay with it.
OR
'My salary expectations are in line with the current industry standards, according to my experience and qualifications.'

Question: 'If you won Rs 20 crore in a lottery, would you still work?'

Sample answer: 'Of course I will work. As already discussed, I am here to craft and design a beautiful future for myself. It is not just about money. Only if I work in a professional setup will I be able to hone and sharpen my skills. Of course, I can use that money for other activities. I am a philanthropist and would like to donate that money for some social cause.'

Question: 'Describe a few things that are important for you in a job.'

Sample answer: 'Any job I work must have two elements—dignity and growth. And the rest will follow.'

Question: 'If I ask you to rate me as an interviewer on a scale of 1 to 10, what will be my score?'

Sample answer: 'Really [smile], I don't think I would be able to do that. You are far more experienced and knowledgeable in this field. All I can say is that I enjoyed talking about myself and the company. It was a learning experience. Also, you are doing an incredible job, Sir/Ma'am.'

Question: 'Do you have any questions for me?'
Please don't say no—always prepare some questions beforehand; it's your chance to talk and get some answers from the HR/interviewer.

And this is actually the wrap of the interview, so do ask a few good questions and get some information about your job profile or the company.

Sample answer: 'Could you please tell me more about this role/position?'
    OR
'Could you please share more about the day-to-day responsibilities of this position?'

Question: 'Why would you want to work for this company?'
Be sure of the USPs of the organization as well as its tagline or vision and mission statements. The latter reflects the company's culture. Also, keep in mind your role and job profile, to give an apt answer.

I would like to share an anecdote that still makes me nostalgic as it was the first-ever interview of my life. In 2001, GE Capital International Services (GESIC) had come for an on-campus recruitment drive to St Ann's College for Women in Hyderabad. In the first introductory round, they made it very clear that we had to tell them something about ourselves and also give a reason as to why we wished to work with GECIS.

I had prepared a little bit about my introduction, but why GECIS—I was very unsure of this. I was a bit nervous as well, and then then all of a sudden I recalled their tagline—We bring good things to life. I even remembered watching their ads at that time.

So, after my introduction, I continued with: 'As your company and products promise to bring good things to life, I am sure if I get a chance to be associated with GECIS, it will bring in many good things to my life as well (professionally).' I ended my answer with my confident smile.

The HR team was very happy, though I was not sure of the merit of my answer!

The next day when I came to college, I was so glad to see my name on the 'selected candidates' list. So, surely that tagline had saved me!

So, knowing about the company, their products and services always help.

Sample answer: 'I would like to work for your company because it is known for its great professional leaders and it is doing a tremendous amount of good work even for society. Other than that, the main reason is my job role—it will give me an opportunity to learn and share my knowledge as a true professional.

Question: 'Do you believe in out-of-the box thinking? Share with me an instance when out-of-the-box thinking helped you come up with a solution to a difficult problem.'

Well, some terms are cliché—overly used and applied by

everyone. Refrain from using these.

While everybody was busy using the term 'out-of-the-box thinking', I decided to check out the meaning of the phrase 'inside-the-box-thinking'. Believe me, it is much more powerful than the former, as it is always good to stay away from competition and go one step ahead of it. So, inside the box thinking works very well; it boosts your confidence and helps you shine with positive inner strength, ideas and thoughts.

In my dictionary, it means getting to know yourself first, before setting out to conquer the outside world. This approach helps you stay calm and composed, understand the situation well, view the problem, study its cause, and then work from there to combat it.

This is a very unique way to look at a problem by taking into consideration both inside-the-box and outside-the-box approaches.

Sample answer: 'Well, to master out-of-the-box thinking, I strongly believe that we need to assess the situation by looking at it from inside-the-box. This is rarely done. I think it shows that my problem-solving approach is from inside-out. It has always helped me.

For instance, in a college event when we faced a financial crunch, I, along with a few team members, were able to come up with cost-effective ideas after looking into the problem from the grassroots level. We went back to the beginning stage and re-planned the event, by cutting cost in each stage of the entire process. Finally the event took place smoothly without needing more money from external sources.'

Question: What if you are not selected for this job?

This is a tricky question, so be smart and throw in some positive attitude and shine like a star.

Sample answer: 'Well, I am a very positive person and a great learner; however, I wonder why I am asked this question. [Pause, with a positive smile.] In any case, my answer would be this: even if I am not selected, I am a good learner—I will learn from this episode of my life and move on.'

Question: 'What can you offer us that someone else cannot?'

Be your own salesperson. Share your USP, but keep it close to the job profile and throw it in with a dash of attitude! Answer confidently and KISS.

Sample answer: 'I am positive that the energy I bring with me is my USP. Other than that, the kind of skills and knowledge that I possess for this role make me a perfect fit.'

Question: 'What makes you happy?'

Sample answer: 'Well, I am a happy person and small achievements—and not just big success—makes me happy. For instance, achieving all the things in my to-do list keeps me happy and motivated. But I am able to make it big because small things keep me happy and ignited to achieve big things.'

So we come to a wrap here.

There can be so many other questions—the list is endless. However, I am sure that this compilation includes some of the most frequently asked HR interview questions. These questions will help you ace not just in your next HR interview round but will also help you stay positive in life.

A Few Quick Reminders

If you get asked any other tricky questions that we have not discussed here, just keep in mind:

- Stay relaxed and don't panic.

- Listen, and if you do not understand a question, ask for clarity. You can say: 'Sorry, I didn't get you,' or 'Could you please repeat that for me, I didn't get it.'
- Your attitude is more important than just the answers — be positive and upbeat. Carry a small diary to take notes, in case the HR gives you some information about the job role or company.
- Please invest in a good pen. Most of us do not give importance to these small things but they carry a lot of weight. If you can spend so much on other things, why not save some money to get the right stuff for writing — you should own a good but not necessarily expensive pen. Start saving up to get at least one Parker or Cross pen.
- Invest in yourself, but not too much. If you are spending on other unnecessary things and you have just graduated or started earning, invest the money in good-quality accessories. These are generally noticed by people. For example, a good watch and a pen is a must. For young women professionals or students, it is also mandatory to invest in a good handbag. Make sure you keep it clean and away from dust because it is of no use when you buy an expensive product and leave it to grow dusty and grimy.
- Be on time.
- Practice well and add your attitude and positivity to the interview.

19

How to Handle Appraisals

> *The true measure of the value of any business leader and manager is performance.*
>
> —Brian Tracy

What Are Appraisals?

Before I became an HR head, I remember defining appraisals as either a catastrophe or a celebration. If appraisals were positive, they were no less than a celebration, but if they weren't, they could be catastrophic.

But, over the years, I have learnt that there is a lot more to the appraisal process. I understood this when I conducted my very first appraisal as an HR Head along with the entire HR team and functional heads in the organization.

I clearly understood then that appraisals are not just a long and tedious process, but a continuous one.

The most important part of my experience was learning why appraisals are done.

Appraisals are not only done to give away rewards, recognitions and promotions. Rather, it is through appraisals that the journey of an organization can be measured and improved; it is a great tool for the overall development of the employees, systems and the organization as a whole.

A lot goes into it than just scores and ratings. As an organic process, it helps team members, managers and top executives to review past goals, measure them and also communicate and set new goals to achieve higher targets and improve the overall performance of the organization.

Role of HRD in the Appraisals

Most employees are scared and sceptical about performance appraisals because they are not aware of the entire process. This is a big hurdle for organizations as it clearly shows the disconnect between the HR department and the employees.

It is the primary responsibility of the HR department to clearly communicate in detail the entire process to the employees, and it should be made a part of the induction presentation. Employees should be made aware of details such as:

1. Frequency of the performance appraisal—whether the company adheres to annual performance appraisals or half-yearly or quarterly.
2. Explanation of the forms to be filled during appraisals.
3. An explanation of the importance of goal setting.
4. Type of appraisal, and the process to be followed by the respective functional head or departmental head.
5. Ways to have a positive attitude towards the entire appraisal process, especially while receiving feedback from the manager.

Once the HR department provides clarity on these points, it becomes very easy to conduct performance appraisals.

Quick Tips to Handle Appraisals in a Positive Manner

Here are a few time-tested tips that will help you handle the appraisals process like a pro.

1. *Opportunity to learn*: When you look at appraisals as a journey for improvement, you can learn and grow from

it. Do not see this process as a regular exercise; rather, see it as an opportunity to openly receive fresh ideas, set new targets and attain new heights. Do not limit this exercise to just a regular activity by the managers. This is not only an opportunity to learn and get feedback but also a golden chance to clearly communicate your worth to your senior. So, if you go with a positive attitude to learn and grow, you can always connect well and communicate what you want to do for the organization.

2. *Prepare in advance*: You should always prepare for this opportunity to talk and discuss with your senior. Not preparing is akin to letting go of this wonderful opportunity. Let us look at the few things you should be ready with before going for a one-on-one chat with your manager:
   - Do a self-audit. Be ready with your list of achievements and accomplishments. Also keep a note of the responsibilities you have taken up.
   - Know where you need support to contribute more as an employee.
   - Keep a list of questions ready that you need to ask your senior.
   - Be willing to listen to all types of feedback. Prepare yourself mentally.

3. *Take responsibility*: In an appraisal, you will get feedback on your work. The meeting usually starts with your positives, so accept them and say a polite thank you in return. The tough part is the next bit when you are told of the areas you were lacking in. Remember, this will always be a part of your appraisal meeting—accept it and make a note of these points where you need to improve.

4. *Review goals*: This is the most essential part of the appraisal. It is where you review your goals and your efficiency is

measured on the basis of your achievement of these goals. So be ready to review each goal clearly and create new goals once you've accomplished the older ones. Keep moving ahead to achieve higher targets and improve your productivity.

5. *Take notes and make a list of positives*: Sometimes the entire appraisal process gets so emotional that we tend to get carried away and miss out on some key points. Do not let this happen. Make a note of the key issues of your performance — these are usually expressed clearly by the supervisors — and do not miss out on this chance to openly discuss critical issues of your performance. Another reason why you should take notes is that it helps you to stay calmer and keep the discussion focused and to the point.

6. *Not a one-way process*: While taking notes, do not forget that you are free to talk, communicate and express your ideas too. You must speak up if you feel that your supervisor's points are not relevant. It is important to be assertive if you find yourself being bossed over.

7. *Fighting excess emotions*: Many a time I have seen employees break down during appraisals. For those extra-emotional employees, carry tissues with you. But the best thing would be to prepare well, stay mentally strong and if possible, do a dummy practice session at home before your appraisal day. Always bear in mind that an appraisal is an opportunity to learn and improve your craft, so stay cool.

20

How to Improve Your GQ

> *Believe that you possess a basic goodness, which is the foundation for the greatness you can ultimately achieve.*
> —Les Brown

Have you ever noticed that there are people who have an aura of positivity around them. No matter when you meet them, they seem happy and always in control.

I define such human beings as people with a high goodness quotient (GQ).

Even if you don't know them very well, they make you feel good because of the way they treat you and speak with you. They seem to be totally disconnected from fears, frustration and disturbances of our fast-paced life.

I will admit that I am really very low on the scale of GQ. I tend to lose my peace of mind within seconds and just one thing out of my planned list can make me go crazy and just a single word of opposition can make me grow red in anger!

I still have to learn a lot, so, I decided to study a few great men and women around me who scored 10 on 10 for GQ.

Let us unleash the secrets behind GQ and be our best selves. I am sure each one of us wants to be a better version of ourselves. So let us dive straight into some quick tips to improve our GQ.

1. *Love yourself*: Sounds contrary to what I was proposing—making others feel good when they meet you and talk to you. Most of us believe that we should love everyone, and the strange thing here is, we do not include ourselves in the 'everyone'. Most of us tend to be very harsh on ourselves most of the time and end up over-criticizing ourselves. This, in turn, brings sadness, but we are somehow trained not to show it and we keep trying to spread sunshine and smiles. But how can we truly spread happiness if we are short of it? You need to understand that you cannot spread these feelings unless you have them in plenty.

   So what are the steps to fill our empty hearts?

   It's okay not to be perfect. We all are humans—no one can be perfect all the time, so it is okay not to be up to the mark sometimes. It could be a fault in one's dressing sense or work or anything else on a particular day. So don't always look for perfection because this is a journey of self-improvement. It is okay to fall and then rise again.

   Remember the beautiful phrase, 'This too shall pass.' Everything is momentary; nothing is forever. Be it a sad moment or a happy one, keep your emotions in control, as this time will also fly away.

2. *Do small things beautifully and peacefully*: This could be something as simple as talking politely or listening to someone else, rather than just talking about yourself and putting your point forward.

3. *Don't show off and wear no mask*: Only the one who wears a mask thinks that nobody knows he is wearing it! In reality, it is the other way round—the entire world will know that you are not being true. So don't waste precious time in wearing masks, just be you—be real and keep improving. Be a better version of yourself with each passing day,

rather than trying to ape others.
4. *Meditate*: To be high on GQ, one needs to be in control, and for that you need to have a positive mindset. Meditation helps with this and will lay the foundation for a peaceful life. Setting aside some time for meditation every day can bring you back on the right track. Meditation helps remove distractions and to stay focused on what you really want to achieve; it kind of works like a self-audit system—something mandatory for understanding flaws. So, keep this self-audit system in place and practise it regularly to improve your GQ.
5. *Be more empathetic*: This is a very rare quality; there are very few people who really truly are compassionate and considerate in their feelings for others. Don't look out for such people; be one, so that this quality is not rare any more.

21

How to Get Smarter Quicker

Be smart, but never show it.

—Louis B. Mayer

Have you ever come across people who advise you to be smarter even though you are good at your job? They may say that you don't possess worldly knowledge to live and enjoy life fully.

I have heard some statements like, 'You are a very good human being, but you need to get smarter to know the ways of the world!'

So, let us gear up to get smarter in just 21 days.

Believe it or not, we all have the power to change ourselves positively, and overcome any fear in just 21 days.

21 Days Mind Conditioning Theory

This theory was propounded by American surgeon Maxwell Maltz in his book *Psycho Cybernetics* published in 1960. In this self-help book, he suggests that it takes only 21 days to form a new habit and get rid of an old habit. So one could improve one's self-image in 21 days, and many personality development experts including Tony Robbins and Brian Tracy endorse this theory.

According to this theory, you can succeed in achieving your goal in just 21 days if you do not give up that good habit and constantly work towards it.

Many a time we start a new habit, but after a couple of days we feel we cannot do it because of some excuse or the other. These excuses will be big hurdles in your life, so do not give up, and keep on working relentlessly towards your goal. If you succeed in doing a particular task for the first 21 days, you become unstoppable.

Let us begin our five-step journey towards becoming smarter than ever before.

1. *Travel*: As a very popular quote says, 'those who do not travel read only page of life'. I wholeheartedly endorse this statement and encourage all young professionals to take this quote really seriously. If you want to become smarter and learn the ways of the world, just pack your bags once in a half year and go out on a trip abroad. If you can't go abroad, just travel out of your city or state. And it is even better if you travel alone. Try to know people from different places, connect and communicate with them, find out some good restaurants and hotels, manage all by yourself and I can guarantee you that you will come back home smarter, and with many stories to share.
2. *Read*: This is a dying hobby today, but was once a favourite across the world. I find that today's generation is not attracted by good books and stories any more, and prefers to hang out with their digital companions—books are becoming relics of the past. But I strongly believe that reading is essential for three reasons:
    - It improves our emotional connect with others, and this feeling is vital for human development, especially for children. Children should be encouraged to read from a very young age. This will allow them to develop empathy, which is a rare and much-needed emotion in the modern world.

When we read good books, we tend to know and relate with many characters and understand their feelings and emotions, and as we do this, it helps us to also define our own feelings clearly and know ourselves best.

- Books make us think and improve our cognitive skills. Unlike digital and electronic gadgets where the information is processed and fed to our senses, books help us to unlock these senses as one begins to imagine the character, the scenario and sometimes even tries to find solutions to the problem presented. A lot of mental rehearsal takes place while we read, hence reading books can stimulate those locked senses and makes us great problem solvers too, other than making us smarter.
- Books improve and enrich our minds with vocabulary, and hence we can support and convey our feelings properly. In today's world, communication is the key to success, so we cannot afford to not read books.

3. *Stay up to date*: One is considered smarter when up to date. Be it the latest update in whatever field or technology, national politics or international politics; being aware of our surroundings makes us confident and aware. Keep abreast of the things happening around—don't give excuses such as 'I hate politics so I am not aware of this issue' or 'my area of interest is confined to XYZ'.

4. *Work on your strengths (USP)*: The best of leaders do this. Warren Buffet suggests that we should all become masters of our crafts. Try to learn and grow in your field of interest. That way nobody can beat you on your chosen path. Rather than becoming a Jack of all trades and master of none, it is better to gain complete knowledge in one

area. To know that one area where you can grow and challenge others, you have to know what your strengths are. Once you know this, stick to it, polish your craft and keep working at it.

A simple tool to know your strength is to do a SWOT analysis. Refer to Chapter 15 for more on this.

5. *Manage your time wisely*: We all have limited resources and limited time; however, only a smart individual is able to make the best use of his time. The trick behind this is to live a life of discipline. So be disciplined, and get the most out of your time. Discipline will act as a bridge to reach your goals. Discipline will stop things from getting chaotic and confusing.

Activity Time

Let us now assess how much smarter you have become after reading these tips!

Read everything carefully before writing/doing/saying anything. Then, fill in the details below.

Name: _____
Age: _____
Sex: _____
Occupation: _____
Solve 6 + 5 + 4 - 3 - 4 = _____

1. Without feeling shy, say loudly: 'She Sells Sea Shells at the Sea Shore.'
2. Loudly tell your neighbour your best friend's name.
3. Stand up and raise your left arm.
4. Write your name, age and occupation at the top (in CAPITAL letters only).
5. Say your name out loud.
6. Loudly say the word 'YES' five times.
7. Who wrote the book *Wake up to VaKE*?
8. With a big smile on your face, say loudly: 'Hello Anu!'
9. How did you come to know about this programme by Loyal International?
10. Tell everyone the current market rate of the American dollar in Indian rupees.
11. Stand up and sit down three times.
12. What is your definition of happiness?
13. With energy, say loudly, 'Ha, Ha, Ha, Hi, Hi, Hi, Hu, Hu, Hu.'
14. What do the 'three Es' in communication mean?
15. Pat your neighbour's shoulder gently.

Having read till here, now you are required to ONLY answer

questions 5 and 15.

While communicating, do not react. Stop, Think and Act.

How was your experience in this communication exercise?

Remember: *It is not necessary to work hard, always, but very essential to work sharp and smart.*

•

Sometimes we need an extra push to follow our dreams. Words and quotes inspire me. You too can dig up some good books and get some motivation from them. However, when I need motivation, I like to write — sharing with you a few lines from my poems.

I am Ink
I am Ink,
I am born to leave an impression,
 (which will force you to think.)

And remember...
You can't scare me,
You can't stop me.

You can't erase, wipe or rub my existence.
And,
Whenever you try to use,
(abuse and shatter my persistence)
I will ink more and more as I was born to spread ideas and leave a deep impression.
This ink will surely empower the revolution.

And the more I ink, the more...
You reach to the brink
Of your false ego, pride and jealous.

I see you getting weak to see the truth

(standing at the peak.)

Coloured in my soul, tears and pain
My words for sure today will become
my weapons, strength and my way.

Be a Warrior
I am the revolution,
I am the power.
As I await none, no friend no follower,
The truth is simple, we are all single.
Be a warrior; be a champion;
(be the light and win your own fight.)
This is my attitude, you may take it otherwise.

Incantation of Ink
Words let me fight,
Without the swords and knives.
It peels the skin and touches,
The heart, soul and mind.
I write sometimes to touch,
Sometimes to kill not the person,
But the bitter design of your instinct,
Conspiring against me.
I wish that these athletic words built,
Can shed the acrimony,
And make you think,
To make the bond dulcet, pleasant and sweet.
How wonderful everything would be,
Only if we all could see, feel and use the,
Incantation of ink.